Captive of the Crime Queen

THE UNDERWORLD DUET
BOOK ONE

PERSEPHONE BLACK

CONTENT WARNING:

This is a Mafia romance, which means there's a cavalier attitude to things like murder and crime, and our heroines get their hands bloody, too.

The book contains references to human trafficking, kidnapping, gun violence, knives, murder, physically and emotionally abusive parents, domestic / intimate partner violence (not between our heroines), abuse of power/Stockholm Syndrome, and threats of sexual violence from an antagonist.

Reader discretion is advised.

CHAPTER 1

Aurora

BEFORE

A SOFT BREEZE rustled through the trees as I meandered home from school, taking my time along the winding path through the park. I loved being surrounded by nature, no matter the season. In fall I enjoyed the vibrant reds and oranges of the changing leaves, the earthy scent of the soil. In summer, the sun was a warm caress when I lifted my face up to it. Even in winter, the gentle crunch of icy grass under my boots made me feel at peace.

But something felt different about this spring day. Not even the most gorgeously bright red geraniums in the flower boxes of the diner down the road could lift my strange sense of foreboding. And by the time I reached home, the sun had been veiled by clouds, casting a hazy late-afternoon glow across the sky that threatened to die into darkness soon.

I always made the walk home last as long as possible. Home wasn't really a home for me.

I slipped in quietly through the back door, not wanting to draw attention to my late arrival. But as I crept down the hall, heading for the stairs that would take me up to my bedroom, I heard tense voices drifting from the living room.

"Please, just give me a few more days!" My father's voice, usually so aggressive, sounded small and afraid.

I'd never heard him like that before.

"Hades has given you enough time." The answering voice was female, low and smooth like honey, but with an edge sharp as a knife. "Today is the day you pay your debts, Verderosa."

I peeked around the corner, curiosity winning over caution. My father cowered on the couch, wringing his hands. Opposite him, in the armchair usually reserved for him, sat a woman with hair black as night and eyes like chips of silvery ice. She couldn't have been much more than thirty, but she radiated power and authority.

And she didn't sit like a woman. She sat like a predator tensed before springing, legs wide as she leaned forward, elbows on her knees, those mesmerizing eyes locked with my father's.

"Take the girl!"

The girl? *Me?* He was offering me up to this strange woman?

"No, please! Not my daughter! She's only seventeen!" I heard my mother cry out. She had hurried in to the room from the kitchen, and I could hear the desperation in her voice. "Take this instead. My grandmother's tiara. It's worth far more than Aurora."

There was an agonizing pause.

"Is that what you really think?" came the strange voice at last —so cool and low. "No. I see in your eyes you value your daughter much more than that trinket." I stood frozen in the hallway, heart thudding in my ears as the conversation paused. "But as you say, your daughter is a child," came the smooth voice of the stranger at last. "Hades has no use for children."

"She's old enough to work to pay off my debt!" My father still sounded desperate. "And when she comes of age, Hades can have her in his bed. Just look at her mother—the girl is a rare beauty, too."

Revulsion rose in my throat at his words. He was bargaining me away like chattel, offering up my body…my future. I trembled with fury, nails digging into my palms.

But still I stayed quiet. My throat tightened, strangling my voice.

"The Styx Syndicate does not deal in sex trafficking," the woman responded. "Especially not of children."

My father sputtered protests, but she cut him off.

"I will take your wife's tiara as collateral for now. But I *will* return to collect the full amount you owe Hades. Cowering behind your connections will not save you, Verderosa."

And I stood frozen in the hallway as the dangerous woman rose from her seat and strode to the doorway in heavy leather biker boots, the kind I'd never be allowed to wear myself. Not ladylike, both my father *and* mother would say. There seemed nothing so important in this world than being a lady.

I scurried back from the corner, but not fast enough, so that I was still standing in full view as the woman rounded it. But she ignored me completely, heading for the front door instead, the faint scent of her leathers both foreign and exciting to me— and a spicy perfume under that, the kind that suggested adventure.

Danger.

I breathed in deep through my nose, trying to memorize that scent, and just as she passed by me her odd, pale eyes met mine for a split second that seemed to stretch on…and on.

I was pinned in place by her intense gaze—a butterfly stabbed through, something to be studied. Admired.

I was used to people admiring me. My father always dragged me out in front of company, even company that made my insides churn with the way they looked at me, bragging about my beauty.

The gray-eyed woman was staring at me now, and my

insides churned…but not the way they did when all those male friends of my father's looked at me.

No, this was more like…like turning somersaults in the pool, my stomach flipping over itself as I lost myself in the icy waters of her eyes. Fear tingled through me, but also something more, something that made my skin flush and my pulse race erratically.

My cheeks felt warm. My lips parted, as though I was going to speak. Going to cry out for her to help me, to take her away from this place, to take me on one of those adventures *she* was heading toward.

Her eyebrows, straight black streaks across an unearthly-pale face, rose up a little, the only reaction to seeing me. For a moment we stared at each other…

And then she looked away and swept out the door, tiara in hand.

The night air rushed in, making me shiver despite its warmth, and it did nothing to cool the fire that seemed to have been lit inside me. Distantly, I heard my father's anguished cries as he realized the tiara was now gone, out of his grasping hands.

"You stupid woman!" he raged at my mother. "All these years you've had it, while I struggled and borrowed! Why did you keep it hidden from me?"

My mother's reply was soft, trembling. "It…it was all I had left of my family."

I'd seen the tiara only once before, when I'd been "exploring." Years ago, there was one day when my parents were both out and I was left alone, and I crept into the forbidden basement and poked among the boxes. The basement seemed to me to be where my parents kept the broken things not broken enough to be thrown away, though they never had them fixed.

The broken things just stayed there in the dark, as dust and time crept over them.

And among those broken things I found a treasure. A

sapphire and diamond tiara so bright and gleaming that I'd assumed it was fake, despite the weight.

It had been buried, boxes in boxes, under all the broken things.

Now, I realized, it *had* been real.

But the next time I went to look at it, it had gone, and I never saw it again until that day, swinging casually from the ice-eyed woman's long fingers.

Heavy footsteps stormed across the living room floor and I darted upstairs and into my room, heart pounding, and hid in the closet.

The front door slammed, but I stayed curled up in my closet long into the night, unable to calm my spinning mind. The ice-eyed woman dominated my thoughts.

Her cool confidence, her sharp beauty, the simmering danger that clung to her...

I was terrified of her.

But another part of me thrilled at the memory of those piercing eyes sliding over me, lighting an unfamiliar fire low in my belly. Yes, this woman was dangerous. I knew that instinctively.

And yet I longed for another glimpse of those pale eyes.

I wanted to feel her gaze on me once more.

CHAPTER 2

Aurora

NOW

I STARE at my reflection in the full-length mirror, hardly recognizing the bride looking back at me. The ivory satin and lace of the heavy wedding dress clings to my body, accentuating every curve until it flares into a full, long train. My dark blonde hair is styled into elegant curls, my makeup airbrushed perfection.

I look every inch the blushing bride—except for the dread in my eyes.

When my father told me a month ago, on the day I turned twenty, that he'd arranged a marriage for me, I knew I had no choice. Just like I've never had a choice in anything else. And I knew what it meant: that finally, my father's debts had become too heavy for him, and I was the price for his freedom.

I'd always known this would happen. I'd even secretly hoped sometimes that I'd be turned over to the ice-eyed woman who had come to collect the debt my father owed to the Styx Syndicate. But the years had gone by and the woman had never come to collect, even though my father still hadn't paid off that debt.

And over the last four years, the Styx Syndicate had become the most feared gang in Chicago, violent and untouchable, the kind of people even the Mob were worried about. I knew that because my father's poker games, held down in the basement of our house, often featured important politicians or men high up in law enforcement, even a judge. I would creep halfway down the stairs to the basement and listen to their talk, stories of the things the Styx Syndicate had done—their vicious murders, their cruelties—and those tales made me sick with dread.

And yet I was fascinated, and the gossip from my father and his cronies kept me informed. According to them, this syndicate of mercenaries had greatly increased their power and territory, rivaling or besting the mafia in several areas. I hung on news of them, poring over the internet rumors about their leader, unnamed and never seen. But I didn't really care about Hades, anyway.

It was the woman I wondered about. That ice-eyed woman who worked for Hades and who, despite her threats, had never reappeared to claim the rest of my father's debts.

Those debts had only grown in size and number of creditors, so that eventually, my father had auctioned me off to the highest bidder, which turned out to be the heir to the Imperioli Family.

He was a man who made my skin crawl, my soul cold. During our one and only meeting, when Nero Imperioli looked me up and down, chuckling as his eyes devoured me, I felt ill enough to have to excuse myself to the kitchen, where I leaned over the sink, trying not to vomit.

But there was no use protesting. I knew that. So I kept my mouth shut, and now…

Now here I am, about to marry a monster.

I hear a small gasp behind me as my mother enters the room where I've been dressing, above the chapel. Her eyes are rimmed red from crying. She moves to straighten my veil, her fingers trembling. "You look beautiful, darling," she says, but her voice cracks with emotion. "But here—let's replace this cheap thing."

She plucks the plastic tiara from my head, the one the bridal shop supplied, and takes out a blue velvet box, holding it out to me to open it, which I do, and then suck in a breath.

A tiara of silver, sapphire and diamond—and real, or real enough to fool. I know it must be fake, though, because the original went off with the gray-eyed debt collector several years ago, the woman who made my father cower before her.

Even now I remember those eyes of hers. I didn't feel nauseated when *she* looked over me.

The tiara is heavy on my head, as heavy as the words my mother says to me now as she helps me arrange it with my veil. "This is for luck," she murmurs. "You know the saying. It's something old, but also something new—to you, at any rate. Something borrowed, and the sapphires are blue."

I force a small smile, wanting to reassure her. "Thank you, Mama."

And then my mother embraces me tightly, whispering fiercely in my ear. "You need to stand up for yourself, Aurora. Don't just give in to everything. I know you want to keep the peace, but being so accommodating will only lead to more pain."

An unfamiliar sense of anger floods me at her words. I'm not the only one who has only ever submitted to my father's wishes.

Who else have I learned it from, if not from her?

But I know she's right. I've spent my whole life being agreeable, avoiding confrontation, telling people what they want to hear. It was the only way to keep my father happy.

And now I'm paying for his mistakes.

I'm twenty-one, and when I look around, I see so many other twenty-one year olds who run their own lives. They live in apartments on their own, or with friends. They have exciting jobs that their college degrees opened up for them, and they buy their own cars or know how to travel on the bus or train without getting hopelessly lost, and they date, they have friends, they have...

They have lives.

And I want so badly to be like them, but I'm too scared all the time. Too scared to even try. My father kept me helpless all these years…and I let him.

A sharp knock on the door startles Mama and me, and before I can respond, the door swings open. Nero Imperioli strides in, his hulking frame filling the doorway. He's impeccably dressed in an elegant black tuxedo, but his stony eyes and cruel smile make him look more like the mobster he is than a groom.

"Get out," he barks at my mother. Her mouth opens, a protest on her lips, but like me, she's been too well-trained all these years. With one last, worried glance in my direction, she scurries from the room.

Nero's eyes rake over me again, a leer twisting his mouth. "Well, you clean up nice," he chuckles. "Can't say I'm disappointed with my purchase."

I suppress a shudder, and I try my best to do what my mother said I should do. "Nero," I begin, only a tiny shake in my voice, "although I did not choose this marriage, I hope we can make the best of it and work together as partners."

In an instant, his hand shoots out and grabs my throat, shoving me back against the wall. I choke against his hold, pinned by his hulking frame looming over me.

"Let's get one thing straight, princess," he growls. "I'm your master now. You'll serve me dutifully as my wife, on your back, on your knees, however I desire it, and I'll breed a new generation on you. Other than that, I have no use for you. And for the rest of your goddamn life, I don't want to hear you speak unless I ask you a direct question. Got it?"

He releases me and I slump to the floor, coughing and shaking. Nero sneers down at me. "Pathetic. But you sure do look pretty all dolled up. Make sure you're smiling big in the wedding photos. Your looks are why you cost so much, and I want to make sure I get value for money."

With that he turns and stalks out, the door slamming behind him. I stay huddled on the floor, sobs rising in my aching throat as I contemplate the nightmare my future holds.

But I can't let myself dwell on what's to come. I just need to get through today. Through the wedding night...

Slowly, I pick myself up off the floor and mechanically fix my smeared makeup, clearing my mind of all thought.

A second sharp rap of knuckles on the door sets my heart racing again, but then I hear my father's voice. "Aurora! It's time. Open this door so I can get a look at you."

I smooth my hands over the lace and silk of my wedding dress and paste a bright smile on my face before I open the door.

My father walks in, then looks me up and down critically. "You'll do." His hand clamps down on my arm in a painful grip. "Remember to thank all the guests for their gifts and blessings, girl. And you make sure you please your husband tonight, you hear me? I don't want to hear any complaints from him."

I've never been with a man. Never wanted to be. The only romantic stirrings I've ever felt were for my best friend Sophia in high school. We used to practice kissing in her bedroom after school, fumbling and giggling until Sophia's mother called her for dinner and sent me home.

Sophia dumped me without explanation when she got her first boyfriend.

And I never had the courage to pursue romance after that early heartbreak. What good was romance, anyway, when it meant my mother had ended up with someone like my father?

Now here I stand, about to be married off to a violent

stranger. I feel nothing but cold fear at the thought of him touching me, possessing the virtue I never cared to protect. I've never thought much about my virginity before, but even if I had, my body is not mine to give.

It's only a bargaining chip for my father to trade.

I wish…oh, I *wish* I could have taken some pleasure for myself before being condemned to a life serving my father's greed. But I'm hollow inside, an obedient daughter too timid to seize the joy that flickers at the edge of my vision. The only sparks of longing I've felt were in those stolen moments with Sophia.

And once more, when that ice-eyed woman looked at me— looked at me and really *saw* me. The first time anyone had seen beyond my face and into my soul.

My father yanks me out of the room, down the hallway to the foyer, where I can hear the wedding guests beyond the grand closed doors, their laughter and chatter. I feel faint and put my free hand against the wall to steady myself. My father's nails dig into my arm.

"Smile, Aurora! Get that sour look off your face, girl. I won't have you embarrassing me." I force my lips to curve and blink back tears as we stop before the huge wooden doors leading into the chapel.

There are two attendants standing at the doors. One of them, a blonde woman with dark eyes, is looking hard at me. I hope she can't see that I've been crying.

I hope she doesn't see the marks on my throat.

I don't catch her eye. I don't want to see the look of pity—or worse, contempt. But when I give her a nervous glance, she's staring instead at my veil, the tiara on my head. She turns to the man standing with her, her fellow attendant, and nods. Together, they pull open the heavy doors that lead to the inner chapel.

Beyond those doors, a sea of unfamiliar faces turn to me,

their eyes bright with anticipation for the show. My knees go weak but my father's grip keeps me upright as he pulls me into the aisle.

Then I see the flowers. Creamy roses and lilies arranged beautifully along the pews, their sweet perfume rising. Snowdrops, white hyacinth, baby's breath. I name each one in my mind like a mantra, using their beauty as a focal point to keep panic at bay.

My father's punishing hold urges me along faster than I can gracefully go in my heels. I stumble a little, but he wrenches me upright. "Smile," he hisses, though his own teeth are bared in a terrible rictus grin.

Roses. Lilies. Snowdrops. Hyacinth. Baby's breath.

I make my lips stretch wider, blinking back humiliated tears, as we proceed toward the altar where Nero waits. His coarse, heavy face is flushed with liquor and anticipation, and his best man leans in to say something that makes him grin lewdly at me.

Roses. Lilies. Snowdrops. Hyacinth. Baby's breath.

The guests are all strangers to me, watching this ritual with avid eyes. And I am a lamb led to slaughter. An innocent thrown into the arena with a lion.

There's only ever one way those stories end.

As we reach Nero, my father's grip loosens and he steps back, his task complete. I glance to the guests seated in the front pews, and find them all male, all cruel-eyed. These are Nero's men, here to bear witness that he receives what he paid for. Their eyes crawl over me like insects. I look to the altar and grip my bouquet tightly, determined not to shame myself by weeping. I stare at the flowers and breathe in their perfume, finding calm in their beauty as the priest begins the ceremony.

Just a little longer and this will be over.

Roses. Lilies. Snowdrops. Hya—

With a crash like thunder, the doors to the church smash

open, and a group of men and women march into the hall. They're all dressed in black, all masked—half-masks that cover only the top part of their faces—

They're all bearing weapons. Knives, chains, guns.

And they're headed straight down the aisle toward me.

CHAPTER 3

Aurora

A GASP ESCAPES MY THROAT, but the front row of Nero's men have stood in turn, milling in front of me, barking out orders of protection.

For a crazy moment, I think they're protecting *me*.

But it's Nero they're worried about. Nero they're pushing back. Nero who is refusing to go, bellowing out that this insult will not stand—*who dares interrupt his wedding day*—as his men form a protective circle around him, shoving me aside in their haste.

I stumble, my heel catching on the hem of my dress. No one moves to help me, but I right myself.

And the group who interrupted Nero's wedding day fans out quickly, well choreographed, some surrounding the altar and others stationed to block the exits. There are about twenty of them, I think. And then one of them—a woman with long, wavy blonde hair and a wolf mask—tips her head back and *howls*, howls loud and long like a wolf, the sound raising goosebumps on my arms.

The other masked people are chuckling, but under that, I

hear a murmur through the crowd of guests. They seem to know who she is, though I've never seen this woman before.

"Hello, boys," she says in a singsong voice to Nero's body-guards. "Stand aside. We're not here for your boy. Not today."

Nero snorts in contempt, straightening his tie as he steps forward. "My men will stand their ground. Who the *fuck* do you think—"

The woman laughs, cutting him off, and tilts her head, her widening smile giving her a predatory appearance under the sharp lines of her mask. When she speaks, her voice drips scorn. "Poor little dictator Nero, so ashamed of his manhood that he has to buy himself a virgin bride." Nero's face goes purple. He opens his mouth to respond but the woman continues, "We're here to collect a debt long overdue. This bride doesn't belong to you, sugartits."

"No!" my father cries out. For the first time, I look at him. He's gray-faced, almost frantic. "No, I gave my blessing to Nero—"

"But you'd already given your daughter away, old man," comes a cold, high voice from behind us all. "Or have you forgotten?"

Before Nero can splutter out more than a few choked sylla-bles, the whole chapel turns as one to see a figure appear at the open doors, silhouetted against the light. Tall and imposing, she strolls down the aisle wearing leathers and a motorcycle helmet. With a graceful sweep, she pulls the helmet off, shaking out a mane of messy, silky black hair that falls to her shoulders in a shaggy cut.

And then her silver-gray eyes meet mine, and I gasp.

It's...*her.*

The ice-eyed woman.

Nero's face, reddened with anger, now drains of color. "Y-you!" he chokes out.

The woman says nothing, simply turns her wintry eyes on

Nero, who is sputtering impotently. He takes an involuntary step back.

"Hello, little brother," she purrs, her voice soft, yet edged with steel. "Surprised to see me?"

Nero's throat bobs as he swallows hard. When he speaks, his voice comes out hoarse. "*Hadria*. I thought you were…"

"Dead?" The woman—Hadria, I suppose?—arches one brow. "No, little brother. Just busy building an empire while you played at being Papa's heir. But don't worry; I'm not here to kill you. That day will come, but it's not today." Nero's men bunch around him again, pulling him back, but Hadria doesn't even glance at them. Her gaze has turned back to me. "No," she says calmly. "Today I am only here to collect a debt."

I stare at Hadria just as unblinkingly as she is staring at me. She's as beautiful as she was four years ago, and all I can do is stare, uncomprehending, as Hadria's long, elegant finger points directly at me.

"The bride belongs to me," she says.

My knees go weak. I grab the nearest pew and manage to keep upright.

"What do you mean?" my father demands, though his voice wavers.

Nero's doesn't waver. He rages, rages like a four-year-old who's been told he can't have a toy he's been staring at through the store window. "The girl is mine, fairly bought and paid for!"

"I'm afraid not, little brother," the woman says. "This one was promised to me long ago. Her father made a deal he seems to have forgotten."

And my father splutters again, denials, protests, but his voice fades to nothing in my ears as I look deep into her glacial eyes. She's exactly how I remember her—and so very different. Even harder now, like she's been carved from marble. But I see something there in her eyes, a glimmer of something. It's gone too quickly for me to be sure, but it's enough to make my heart skip a beat.

Nero keeps up his protests, but all at once, Hadria silences him with an icy look. "Enough squawking." He subsides into silence. She crooks her finger at me. "Come here."

I find myself obeying without conscious thought, my feet carrying me toward her. She reaches out and grasps my chin between thumb and forefinger, tilting my face up to examine me. Her touch sends a thrill right through my body.

"Exquisite," she murmurs. "Like a pure ray of sunshine in human form. That fool father of yours was right; you grew into a rare flower."

Her words spark that memory to life, when my father offered me to her. I'd been only a girl then, and she had refused me. But now...

Hadria releases my chin and turns to Nero with a shrug. "You have a problem, take it up with her father."

Fury boils up in my father's face. Hadria—is that what Nero called her?—only looks amused.

"I won't be robbed!" Nero shouts after a moment. "The girl is mine!"

Hadria gives a sigh. "Oh, little brother. When will you learn you can't keep things that don't belong to you?"

"Hadria, you bitch—" he begins through clenched teeth.

"Actually, it's 'Hades' these days," she tells him, and at that name, the whole group of Nero's men sway back, as though for a moment, they're thinking about turning tail and running.

The woman turns to the chapel and raises her voice. "It's time you all knew. I was born Hadria Imperioli, eldest child of Giuseppe Imperioli. But this city knows me as Hades, leader of the Styx Syndicate. And now I've decided it's time to claim what is owed to me. My birthright—the Imperioli Family—every-thing. But I'm starting with this girl, who was promised to me by her father four years ago. And since none of you can do a goddamn thing to stop me, I suggest you get out of my way."

Nero's men begin to move forward again, but Hadria's people surge to meet them. She pulls me close, shielding me as fists and weapons begin to fly.

"Time to go, Sunshine," she murmurs in my ear. The feel of her breath on my skin makes me shiver. She keeps an arm firmly around my waist as she propels us up the aisle, somehow untouched amidst the brawlers. The guests have already fled to the sides of the chapel, screaming and ducking.

Through the foyer, past more panicked people…

And then she sweeps me outside into the bright morning sun and I take the first breath of free air in my whole life.

CHAPTER 4

Hadria

MY HEART IS POUNDING as I hurry Aurora out of the church, her intrusively-large wedding skirts catching on every damn thing we pass.

My heart never pounds. Even when I'm staring down the barrel of a gun, it stays steady and familiar. But it's pounding now.

It's just the adrenaline from stealing my brother's bride right out from under his nose. That must be it. God, the shocked look on Nero's slack face was priceless.

But as we hit the street and I take in Aurora's wide eyes and parted lips, an unfamiliar ache blooms in my chest.

"Are you wearing anything under that ridiculous outfit?" I demand. "A slip, like a good little girl?"

Her eyes are big as dinner plates, and she just nods, until I pull my switchblade from my boot. Then she gasps, takes a step back, but I grab her by the neckline of her dress, pull her close again, and slice right down the front of in one clean motion before she can cry out.

The fabric falls away, leaving her in a slip of white satin. I yank the tiara and veil off her head and jam the motorcycle helmet on instead.

And then I throw my leg over the bike I parked right here on the sidewalk, and haul her onto it behind me.

"Better hold on tight, Sunshine," I call over my shoulder as I rev the engine. Her arms wrap around my waist tentatively, clutching tighter as soon as I peel out, and I savor the feel of her body pressed against my back.

But we're already out of time. Two of Nero's men managed to follow us out, and they're already into their car, the engine starting up.

I race through the city like a demon fleeing hell. I risk a glance over my shoulder to judge the distance, and see Aurora's hair streaming behind her like a damn flag, showing Nero's men the way to go.

But that's not fair. She sure didn't seem to want to marry that asshole.

Who would, after all?

I look ahead again, focus on the road twisting and turning before us, and floor it. The acceleration slams us both down into the seat, my thighs tensing to compensate for the force of gravity. I hurtle around a corner and the roar of the engine echoes off buildings, punctuated by the occasional gun shot from behind.

They finally pulled their dick-substitutes out, did they? Interesting. They probably don't want to kill Aurora, or not on purpose, anyway. But if they hit me, we'll crash, and either way, it'd be game over.

So I push my bike harder, faster, until the wind whips tears from my eyes and drowns out everything else.

We reach an intersection, banked up with traffic. I slow slightly, braking before swerving sharply left, skidding sideways through the crossroads, narrowly avoiding collision with a taxi, while another car clips my rear wheel, causing the bike to fish-tail wildly before I manage to correct course once more.

Now we're heading north, parallel to the river. Up ahead lies a bridge, the bridge I need to get to my first destination, but at least one of Nero's men has picked us up again, his car inching closer.

And up ahead, they've begun to halt traffic in preparation for the bridge to lift and let the waiting boats through.

But I smile. The timing of these lifting bridges was always part of the plan. And I only accelerate as I close the distance, Aurora's arms tightening on my waist.

She doesn't protest. Doesn't scream. She trusts me, I think.

Just before impact, I feather the throttle, sending us surging forward at breakneck speed, just as the road crew waves franti-cally at us to stop—slow down—anything!

And then, without warning, I rear up on the foot pegs, *willing* the bike up and into the air. Aurora moves with me instinc-tively. For a split second, we hover in mid-air, poised precari-ously between success and failure over the barricades and the parked cars in front of the bridge.

Thank God Aurora's such a tiny little thing.

I sail effortlessly over the cars, landing with a solid thump on the bridge, and I gun the engine again as soon as I have control of the bike.

I allow myself a self-satisfied smirk at the awe-struck faces of Nero's men in the mirror, and a moment later, we're across the already-rising bridge, just one more little jump to clear the gap, and then skidding past the barricade on the other side, and zooming away, free.

Nero will not forget this day in a hurry. And neither will our father, when he hears of it. If only he could have been there to see it.

Damn him. Where *was* he?

But I refocus. I can interrogate the terrified little kitten clinging to me once we reach the safe house, find out where her dear intended father-in-law was on her big day.

A few blocks later, we pull into an underground parking garage and I cut the engine. Aurora slides off the bike at once, fumbling at the helmet strap with shaking hands. I pull her close to help her, my fingers brushing against the soft skin of her neck. She inhales sharply at the contact.

"Y-you saved me," she whispers, once I get the helmet off. "Why?"

At that, I laugh, and swing off the bike. "Saved you? Oh, sweetheart."

I seize her wrist and stride toward the elevator, Aurora scrambling to keep up on those stupid-high wedding heels. As soon as the doors slide shut I pin her against the wall, forearm across her collarbone.

"I did not *save* you, Sunshine. I merely reclaimed what was mine. You belong to me now."

She swallows hard but lifts her chin. "I don't belong to anyone."

I press harder, our faces inches apart. Her eyes flash with defiance and I feel that strange ache again. Feel the desire to *force* her to say it, to admit that she's mine, to make her beg and plead for mercy…

No one has dared challenge me in a long time. Well, no one but Lyssa, and she doesn't count. It's her *job* to challenge me.

"You don't belong to anyone?" I give her my coldest smile, and the darkness in me gives a pleasurable little sigh at her flinch. The elevator doors open and I step back. "We'll see about that."

I pull her into the apartment. This tiny weed of a girl might have gotten under my skin just then, but it was only momentary. The adrenaline from that ride through the streets, the close escape. That's all.

I'm in control.

"W-where are we?" she stammers out.

The place is luxuriously appointed, but empty-feeling none-theless, like it's been professionally staged for an upcoming sale. The walls and shelves are bare, devoid of books, photographs, decoration or any personal touches. I can see Aurora staring around, puzzled.

I shut the door and lock it securely, then check the windows, peeking down to the streets below. Doesn't look like we were followed.

Aurora looks around nervously, her eyes darting from one empty corner to another. "Where are we?" she asks again finally, her voice a little louder.

"A safe house," I reply curtly. "The first stop on our journey."

Confusion flits across her face. "Journey? Where are we going?"

"Stop asking questions."

She shivers suddenly, goosebumps rising on her arms. It *is* chilly in here, especially if one is only wearing a slip, I assume.

I shrug off my leather jacket and hold it out toward her. "Here," I tell her. "Put this on."

She looks at me warily but takes the jacket nonetheless, slip-ping it on gratefully as she wraps herself in its warmth. As she pulls it tight around her body, I notice once again how small she is, fragile even, beneath its bulkiness.

I imagine what Nero would have done to her on their wedding night. A strange, icy rage fills me as I picture his violence, his cruelty, his delight in causing pain.

Aurora shrinks back, mistaking my anger as directed at her, and a desire I've never felt before rears up in me: the desire to reassure. I take a breath, try to find unfamiliar words, when I'm thankfully interrupted by a banging on the door that makes Aurora jump.

I cross the room, gun in hand, and slide up next to the door, waiting.

"Lupo," comes a voice from the other side.

I unlock and open the door. Lyssa saunters in, followed by several of my men. They're still hyped up from the action, congratulating each other and recounting their favorite moments. Lyssa's eyes light up when she spots Aurora cowering in my jacket, and she gives that predatory smile of hers.

"You…" Aurora says, recognition dawning. "You were in the foyer. One of the wedding attendants."

"Perceptive," Lyssa drawls. She looks at me. "All clear so far, Boss. Rest of our people are down there, watching the streets."

"Well, well, what do we have here?" drawls Vinny, one of Lyssa's newest recruits. He strides toward Aurora. "Nice view, sweetheart," he leers.

A single glance at Lyssa and she's between them in an instant, her knife against his throat, her eyes on me for the order. I even consider it for a moment. But I reach for my customary cool instead. "You look at her again and you'll lose your eyes," I tell him calmly.

I think it's my calmness that really undoes men like Vinny so easily. They expect fire from their superiors. They don't know how to deal with frost.

Vinny stammers apologies as Lyssa lets him go. "Go and check the perimeter and streets," I tell him. "*Now*." He scrambles to obey. Lyssa sends me an amused, questioning look. I ignore it and grab Aurora's arm. "We're leaving. Let's go."

I want to get us away from here quickly, before my fool brother gets lucky and stumbles across a witness who saw which way I went.

It's time to return home.

Lyssa takes the stairs to make sure they're clear, while I pull Aurora into the elevator again. I stand with my hand firmly around her bicep, such as it is, and stare straight ahead.

I can't bring myself to look at her again right now.

I'm not sure why.

I only know that I might come undone, and that won't do. I need all my focus if we're to get out of the city unharmed.

She's changed since I saw her four years ago—and yet she hasn't changed at all. Physically, she is even more beautiful than I remembered. And yet those wide blue eyes are just as guileless as that day I saw a scared, skinny teenager staring at me with her mouth open as I walked past her. I thought by now she might have grown up a little. But as soon as she asked why I'd *saved* her, I knew she was just as naive now as she was then.

And now she speaks again, her soft voice barely enough to fill the small elevator carriage, but enough to make the thing that's twisting inside me loosen up a little.

"Thank you," she says quietly.

After a moment, I snap, "For what?"

"That man. The way he looked at me…"

She's right. The way Vinny looked at her was unacceptable. I won't have a man like that among my people. I'll speak to Lyssa later; have her deal with the matter. "He won't trouble you again," I tell Aurora.

The elevator doors open and I let go of her arm for a moment so I can push her back gently as I peek out to check the surrounds.

Clear.

"Let's go," I tell her, and I reach back to take her arm again.

But somehow, instead of seizing her arm, my hand finds hers instead, and her fingers slide trustingly into mine, holding tight.

Oh, dear. This little ray of sunshine has no idea at all just how dark her world is about to become.

CHAPTER 5

Aurora

IT'S NOT the motorcycle this time.

And it's not just the two of us. Hadria's offsider, the strange blonde woman who howled in the chapel, is in the car with us. She has a wild light in her eye that scares me, so that when she blindfolds me—at Hadria's nod—I'm almost relieved. But based on the length of the drive, I know we must be far outside the city by now. Hadria sits silently beside me, her breath even, her arm not touching mine.

Where are we going? And what will happen when we reach our destination? But one thing seems certain: I'm still a prisoner. I've only traded one kind of jail for another.

The SUV slows and turns, tires crunching over gravel, and the blindfold is pulled from my eyes.

"You don't want to miss the view," the blonde woman says, giving a wicked smirk. I look away from her nervously and take in the view, like she suggested.

The car has stopped at what I think must be a guardhouse, a little hut, because a man—heavily armed, enough to make me shrink away in my seat—jogs out to open the gate for the SUV.

But it's not just a gate. It's a huge, imposing, black iron-barred *portal* that looks like it'd more properly belong at the entrance to Hell. But once we're through, we proceed down a long, tree-lined driveway, and my heart lifts a little as I see the range of plants and trees.

It's not so bad, maybe. Not if there's all this nature around—

But then a huge hulking house looms into view, more ominous than beautiful. It's enormous, a mansion even, but of such modern architecture that it seems futuristic. My breath catches at the imposing edifice of stone and steel. This…this is a fortress, not a home. A huge, squat box with a roof made of a single sheet of black metal, tipped at an angle, and the windows are all shuttered over with the same material.

What *is* this place?

Lyssa and Hadria exit the car without a word. I follow hesitantly, clutching Hadria's leather jacket around me tightly again as the wind hits me, blowing my hair around, whipping into her face as she turns to take my arm again. She closes her eyes momentarily, breathing in, and I stammer out an apology.

"Come," is all she says, and she pulls me with her. But my impractical bridal heels wobble on the gravel drive, almost make me stumble, and Hadria pauses, glancing down at them.

She gives a nod over my shoulder and, with a shriek, I'm lifted up into the air—into the arms of the driver of the car, a man whose hands, I can't help but notice, have lost several fingers. Hadria just walks on, and the man carries me over to the front steps, where he sets me down.

The massive front door of bronze swings open silently and we step into a grand foyer. Polished concrete floors gleam underfoot, and spotlights spear through my eyes as I glance up to see where the light is coming from. Despite the undeniable architectural accomplishment, it feels desolate. Unlivable.

Just as it seemed from the outside, just as I suspected, this place is a prison.

A woman in black pants and a tailored white shirt appears to take our coats, and then a group of staff appears, filing into the foyer in a line. None of them meet my eyes, gazes skittering away. All except one older woman in a gray dress and neat hair who steps forward with a gentle smile.

"Aurora, this is Mrs. Graves, my housekeeper," Hadria says. "She will show you to your room and ensure you have everything you need."

Mrs. Graves nods. "Welcome to Elysium, Aurora." Elysium? What— "It's a pleasure to have you here," she goes on. "Goodness, you must be chilly. Let's get you into a nice hot bath." Her warm demeanor helps steady my nerves—and oh God, a bath sounds amazing right now.

A bath where I can be alone and set my thoughts straight.

It's been a heck of a day, after all.

I turn to Hadria timidly. Take a deep breath. "M-may I?"

There's a flash in her eyes, but I think she's pleased that I asked permission. Or at least, she inclines her head. "Off you go, Sunshine. I'll come and see you once you're settled in."

The soothing sound of Mrs. Graves' voice keeps me anchored as we make our way up a huge, terrifying floating glass staircase that makes me dizzy when I look down, and then we walk a long hallway with smooth, polished stone walls. She points out various rooms—a library, the music room, a sitting room—but I only catch snippets as I struggle to take in the overwhelming grandeur around me.

Because it *is* grand, despite the cold, brutal nature of the building. I'm sure some famous architect must have designed it. Which makes it all the more a pity that it *feels* so unpleasant.

Finally we reach a set of double doors that Mrs. Graves opens with a small key, and we step inside what she calls my "private rooms." The living area is as large as my parents' entire house, furnished with low couches and chairs in shades of gray or white. Square glass lamps adorn minimalist side tables. Through an archway I can see a massive bed, its pillows fluffed to perfection, the sheets and covers of gunmetal silk, with one Chinese red accent pillow.

The whole place looks like something out of a design magazine, if that magazine was doing a special on interior decoration in Hell.

I look around, approach a window. It's completely black outside, no view at all—those metal shutters that I saw outside have cut off any sunlight at all.

"We don't open the shutters of Elysium," Mrs. Graves says. "Security, you understand." I don't understand. I don't understand any of this. But Mrs. Graves just smiles warmly and goes on speaking. "You must be tired. Let's get you into that bath."

She leads me into the bathroom that adjoins the bedroom, which elicits another gasp from me. Black marble countertops, gilded mirrors, and gleaming platinum fixtures give it the feel of a luxury spa. Mrs. Graves turns on the faucet, releasing a rush of water into the large clawfoot tub. She sprinkles in aromatic bath salts that begin to foam and fill the room with the scent of jasmine.

"There now, I'll give you some privacy. There are panels round about in the walls with a range of buttons—push the one that says 'Kitchen' if you need anything, and ask for me. But do take as long as you like. The mistress will be up to see you in an hour or so."

The mistress?

She must mean Hadria, of course.

Hades?

Whatever.

And then Mrs. Graves is gone, closing the door behind her. I hesitate, noticing there's no lock or latch. But the temptation of the bath is too great. I quickly pull off my slip and undergarments, leaving them in a puddle on the floor. Catching my reflection, I'm startled by the heavily-made-up stranger staring back.

This isn't me.

Rummaging in the bathroom cabinet, I find an array of expensive creams and oils. I clean my face thoroughly, removing every trace of makeup until I feel—and look—like myself again. Sinking into the tub, the hot water envelops me. For the very first time today, I feel the tension start to drain from my body. I take a deep breath and will myself to relax, pushing away thoughts of all that has happened. Right now it's just me, alone with my thoughts in this unexpectedly tranquil moment.

I sink deeper into the soothing water, letting it envelop me as my mind drifts. In the days leading up to the wedding, I wished with all my heart to be saved from this fate. I'd pleaded silently for divine intervention, for *anything* that could prevent me from being trapped in a loveless marriage with a man like Nero Imperioli.

And now, here I am. My wish was granted in the most unexpected way imaginable. I've been rescued from one prison only to be delivered into another, the clutches of this dangerous and enigmatic Hadria. I don't know what she has planned for me…

But I fear this fate may be far worse than the one I just escaped.

If her brother is a man like Nero…

If she really is Hades, the leader of the Styx Syndicate…

If the Styx Syndicate is really as violet and vicious as my father and his poker buddies always said…

I bury my face in my hands, shoulders shaking as I allow myself to weep softly until the bathwater has started to cool, and I feel exposed and vulnerable.

But for now, all I can do is dry my eyes and brace myself.

Hadria said she would come to see me, so I need to collect

myself before she arrives. I saw the amused contempt in her eyes when I asked why she'd saved me. I won't let her make me feel small again.

Taking a few deep, shaky breaths, I step out of the tub and wrap myself in the plush robe that hangs nearby. I move slowly into the bedroom, perching tentatively on the edge of the massive bed.

And I wait for Hadria to appear.

CHAPTER 6

Hadria

THE DAY WEIGHS HEAVILY on me as I sit alone in what the Syndicate has come to call the "war room," brooding over the day's events. I'm a little tired. I'm not used to operating in the daylight hours, and I'll have to be awake all night as usual, too, to ensure Nero doesn't try something even dumber than I already expect from him.

I'm slumped in the large, ornate chair that stands on a dais in front of the large table where we lay our plans—inevitably dubbed "Hadria's throne"—and I rub my nose to try to get rid of that feminine scent clinging to Aurora's hair. I got a big whiff of it when her mane blew into my face as we left the car.

It was nice.

But Elysium isn't a place for *nice* things.

Lyssa saunters into the war room, her usual smug grin in place. "Well, well, look who's got the world at her feet," she chirps, throwing herself into her own chair near the head of the table and looking up at me. "Ah, the faces of Nero and all his goons when we pulled that little stunt. Pure poetry."

She makes a chef's kiss as I fix her with an icy glare,

unamused by her jubilant mood. "Save your glee until we've got what we want."

Her eyebrows shoot up in surprise. "What's eating you, Boss? We threw down the challenge today. *And* there are a few less of Nero's men to trouble us now."

I sigh heavily, my mind still consumed by thoughts of my father's absence. "My father wasn't there to witness it," I confess at last.

"So that's what this is about. But you know what they say—every cloud has a silver lining."

"What's that supposed to mean?"

She leans in, a sly glint in her eyes. "Well, isn't it obvious? That little ray of sunshine named Aurora. She's got you feeling all squishy inside."

My jaw tightens at the mention of the girl's name. "Don't be ridiculous."

Lyssa rolls over in her seat to look at me fully, enjoying my discomfort. "Oh, come on. You can't fool me. I saw the way you looked at her."

I tense up at her teasing, feeling the sting of truth behind her words. "She's just a pawn," I tell her with a dismissive shrug.

Lyssa raises an incredulous eyebrow. "A pretty little pawn that's got you pining, maybe."

"She is…pleasant to look at," I admit.

Lyssa cackles triumphantly as she rises from her seat. "See? I knew it! You be careful, Hades. Don't let her wrap you around that little finger of hers."

"Make yourself useful and go fetch, *Wolf*," I snarl back. She saunters out of the room with a wild laugh, leaving me to wrestle with my mood again, an unfamiliar sensation.

I close my eyes and rub my temples, trying to clear my head after Lyssa's teasing. But she's right about one thing—I have not been quite myself since Aurora came into the picture.

I'm not sure Lyssa realizes just how long ago that was, though.

I lean back in my chair, remembering again that first time I saw her—a fragile little bird caught up in her father's tangled web of debt. A very lovely young woman, with that dangerous kind of beauty that launches ships to war...but she was also more than that.

Those wide, curious eyes. Fearful, but fearless at the same time as she stared at me. I sense again now that there's something else inside her, under all that innocence.

Something...dark, like the darkness that lives in me.

It's a darkness that was cultivated in me from birth. Papa might have refused to give me the keys to the Imperioli kingdom, but he still made me into a force to be reckoned with. Weapons training started before I was of school age. And when I disappeared into the streets as a cold response to his preference for Nero, I found Lyssa...and then I really began to carve out my own legacy of blood and fear.

These days, Hades is a name whispered with reverence and awe in the Chicago underworld. I am the shadow people seek out when they have deeds too dark for even hardened mafiosi to commit. Deeds without honor. Dirty deeds that come at a steep price.

And so with dirty hands, I've found my own place. My own kingdom.

My own throne.

But all behind a mask, because I knew that the people I dealt with—just like my father—would not take a woman seriously. I invented a specter, Hades, a mysterious man whose identity was unknown outside the Syndicate, and I claimed to be working on his behalf, under his orders.

When all the time, I *was* Hades. My power and influence grew, along with the reputation of Hades. The Styx Syndicate is feared, hated, and regularly employed.

But it's not enough. It's not what I was born to, not what I have dreamed of all these years. I want my *birthright*. Leading a group of mercenaries is not the same as leading a mafia Family. I want respect, not just fear.

And I want my father to recognize me. I want him to admit that he was wrong to prefer Nero over me. And to do that, I plan to show him, show the Imperioli Family, how easily I can take the things that Nero thinks are his due.

Aurora was just the first example.

Aurora.

My mind keeps returning to her. She's gorgeous and tempting, and there are so many things I would love to do to her...but I can't afford to get distracted. Not now.

My rivalry with Nero has reached a boiling point. Stealing his bride was a bold declaration of war, along with that revelation of my identity. Now I need to focus on consolidating my power, not fretting about the girl. I've set events in motion that cannot be undone.

Besides, she's mine, now.

I wanted her. I took her. I'll keep her, one priceless possession among countless others.

And I'll turn my mind to other things, like the destruction of my brother.

CHAPTER 7

Aurora

FOR THE THIRD TIME TODAY, a sharp knock at the door sets my heart racing. I steel myself, expecting Hadria's intimidating presence. But when the door swings open, it reveals a different woman—the blonde who helped abduct me earlier today.

She saunters into the room, brown eyes sliding over me as a smirk tugs at her lips. She's slender but muscular and moves with grace, exuding the same dangerous energy as Hadria.

I can see why they're friends.

"Well, aren't you just a golden goddamn sunbeam," she drawls, voice dripping with amusement. "All fresh-faced, pink-cheeked, doe-eyed. I can see why the Boss has taken such an interest in you, little Suzy Sunshine."

A chill runs through me at her words. She paces in front of me slowly, assessing me like a lioness toying with cornered prey. Every instinct screams to flee from this woman, but I won't back down. I force myself to meet her gaze steadily.

It only seems to amuse her more. With a laugh, she turns and stalks from the room, pausing only to throw over her shoulder: "Follow me."

I scurry after her.

What else can I do?

We pass through several identical hallways until I have no idea where I am, and then we enter a large, open room, one full wall of which is lined with bookshelves stuffed with books. At the very end of the room is a huge fireplace, just as tall as I am, but it's not currently lit. In the middle of the room is a long, heavy table, seats clustered around it, and at the head of it, slightly raised up, is a huge, ornate wooden chair, padded with leather.

The rest of this house might be a cathedral to modernity, but this room is different. Almost medieval in feel.

"Welcome to the war room, Suzy," the blonde says. "Take a seat. Over there—" She points to a set of leather sofas over in one corner, near what looks like a wet bar. The sofas are facing each other across a coffee table, and compared to the enormous table in the middle of the room, it's practically cozy.

I sit where indicated, straight-backed, perched on the edge of the seat. And then, to my surprise, Hadria enters the room from a concealed side door, dressed casually in black jeans and a charcoal sweater cut low enough to suggest that she wears nothing else underneath. She's still imposing, despite the change in attire. Her porcelain complexion glows against the dim lighting around us, creating an ethereal effect.

"Leave us," she says flatly to the blonde woman. Without argument, the blonde vanishes. Alone now with Hadria, my nerves jump wildly.

Is this when she kills me?

But she merely goes to the wet bar and brings over two tumblers and a bottle of whiskey to the coffee table. She pours generously into both glasses before handing me one. "Drink," she instructs.

I've never had whiskey before. I've never had *any* alcohol before, for that matter. Is she...trying to get me drunk?

On the other hand, given the circumstances, perhaps a bit of that liquid courage I hear people talking about might help.

I raise the glass to my lips and swallow. Fire explodes in my throat, burning down my esophagus until it hits my empty stomach. I double over, coughing harshly.

"Easy," Hadria warns. "It'll hit harder if you haven't eaten anything recently."

Embarrassed, I nod and sip slower this time. The warmth spreads throughout my body, relaxing muscles previously coiled tight with fear. Maybe this isn't such a bad idea after all...

Hadria sips her drink calmly, watching me closely over the rim of her glass. Those piercing gray eyes won't leave mine. Unnerved, I shift in my seat, averting my gaze toward the bookcases lining the walls. Thick volumes bound in rich leather stand sentinel along every available surface. There are no fun-looking paperbacks or contemporary fiction.

"Aurora," Hadria begins softly, setting her glass aside. Instantly, all my attention focuses upon her. "There are things you need to understand about what happened today. About why you ended up here, rather than married to my brother. And I have some questions for you."

I swallow nervously, fighting the urge to run away screaming. Instead, I force myself to nod, determined not to show any sign of weakness. At least not until I figure out whether she plans to kill me or let me go free.

"Your father owed me money," she continues matter-of-factly. "Several years ago he offered you as payment. Said he'd give you to me so that you could work to pay off his debt. Work in the house and...in other ways."

Bile rises in my throat at these words. "I know. I was a *child*," I whisper harshly.

"Yes. And that is why I refused." Before I can respond further, Hadria holds up a hand. "In any case, your mother intervened.

She gave me her second-most prized possession in lieu of her first."

"The sapphire and diamond tiara," I say.

Hadria nods. "But that tiara was only a fraction of what your father owed. Your father was paying back his debt in tiny spurts now and then. So when I heard that he had sold you to Nero—my brother—I decided that I'd had enough of your father's insults. I returned to claim the full payment for his debt."

"Me."

"You."

I take that in, and then I ask, hesitatingly, "But…why?"

"Why?" Hadria echoes.

"Why did you want me?" I ask, my tongue stumbling over the words. They don't come out as I really mean them. "Why are you doing this? What could you possibly gain from…from stealing me away like you did? Are you—are you going to sell me to some man, like my father did, to cover his debt?"

Her eyes flash, and I shrink back in my seat. But my reaction seems to take her aback, and she drops her eyes for a moment, looking down at her drink. "The Styx Syndicate indulges in a great deal of unpleasant business, but not human trafficking. So, no. I don't intend to sell you, Aurora."

I summon up the dregs of my courage. "Do you plan to k-kill me, then?"

"No."

It can't be. She can't mean to—"Free me?"

That provokes a small smile. "Of course not."

I swallow. "Then…what?"

"I intend to *keep* you. You belong to me now, Aurora. You are mine, just like this house, these lands, just like all of Chicago will belong to me in time. You're a symbol to the world of my reach. My power."

Her words dredge up such a whirlwind of feeling that I can't speak. Dread. Disgust. But desire, too…

You belong to me now, Aurora.

I should feel only despair, should rage against the idea, but somehow—

Hadria continues on, oblivious to the churning inside me, outlining the rules of what she calls Elysium, her estate, this gilded cage I'm now trapped within.

Curfews, restricted areas, scheduled meals. Each sentence she speaks brings a new restriction on my freedom.

"And you will find that here, in Elysium, we follow a different schedule. We sleep during the day—usually. And we work at night. In fact, you should feel honored that I got out of bed just to fetch you today, Sunshine."

I say nothing. Stare mutely. She just gives a small smile.

"And you will come to follow a similar schedule. The days are for dreaming. The night is when we come alive. Now, follow my rules, and you'll be treated well," Hadria finishes. "But if you try to escape, or contact the outside world—" She lets the threat hang.

I nod mutely, throat tight. "But…what am I supposed to do while I'm here?" The words sound feeble even to my ears. This woman has kidnapped me, dragged me into a new nightmare, and I still somehow hope for leniency? For mercy? I might as well wish for wings to fly away from this hellhole.

"Do?" Hadria repeats, arching an eyebrow. "Whatever you please." She waves a dismissive hand. "Read, watch TV…"

My jaw drops open involuntarily. Read? Watch TV? While I'm locked up in this place with no view of the outside world, not even an atom of sunlight? Is she serious?

Anger boils in me, threatening to overflow. But then I think better of it. I don't want to provoke her. Not yet, anyway; not before I understand this place. So instead, I manage a timid, "Can I explore the house? The gardens?"

She considers this for a moment, tapping her lip with a perfectly manicured nail. Then she smiles – a cruel, humorless thing devoid of warmth. "Exploring the mansion is permitted," she says slowly. "However, as I said, certain areas are off limits. You wouldn't want to accidentally walk into one of our meetings here in this room, would you?" There's an edge to her voice, warning me not to push my luck too far. "As for going outside..." Her expression hardens. "Absolutely not. You belong to me, Aurora, but there are people who will try to steal you from me. So you will stay in the house at all times."

I want to ask: *For how long?*

But I'm afraid of the answer.

Defeated, I slump back in my chair. Panic claws at my insides, threatening to consume me whole. Trapped here forever, without any access to fresh air or sunlight?

I'm not going to survive this.

"My father—Nero's father—wasn't there at the wedding," Hadria is saying. I lift my head a little, dull eyes focusing on her. "Do you know why?"

That's one thing I actually *do* know, because my father was very angry about it, and I'd hoped for a very brief period that it might save me. "Don Imperioli didn't approve," I whisper.

"Of *you?*" She gives a scoffing laugh. "A pretty little virgin with Italian blood. What more could Papa have possibly asked for, as far as Nero went?"

I swallow. "I think...he thought I wouldn't be..."

"Ah," she says, and her eyes travel me head to foot again. "He thought you wouldn't be tough enough. Well, the old man was right about that." I stare hard at the coffee table, because I know she's waiting for a reaction. "That's all for now," Hadria says at last, standing up. "You may go—back to your room, I think. I'll have food sent up to you."

She turns and leaves before I do.

I sit for a moment in a daze, my mind spinning. I'm not even sure where my bedroom is in this place—it's so big, and all the corridors are the same dark, polished concrete. But when I step into the hallway, the blonde woman leans casually against the wall outside, examining her nails.

"This way, Suzy," she drawls, pushing off and striding down the corridor without looking back.

I scurry to catch up, trying to memorize the route. Left, right, through an arched doorway, then another corridor... But it's no use. The house is a labyrinth of identical hallways and closed doors.

And we pass window after window, all shuttered against the outside.

"Do the windows stay covered *always*?" I ask tentatively.

The woman—Lyssa, I think I heard Hadria call her—snorts. "You heard her. Boss prefers to run her kingdom in the dark. And she doesn't want anyone setting eyes on *you*, little sunbeam."

We arrive at the double doors that I recognize from earlier, and Lyssa shoulders them open to reveal the suite Hadria assigned to me.

My jail cell.

"Home sweet home," Lyssa quips. With an ominous wink, she pivots and stalks away. The doors swing shut behind her with an air of grim finality.

She doesn't lock it. But I have no desire at all to go back out and wander around. I'll just get lost, and then—probably —punished.

I think back to Hadria's cold gray eyes, her imposing demeanor. She *kidnapped* me, and yet I feel a pang in my chest. Pity for someone who surrounds herself with darkness and solitude. What traumas lurk in her past, shaping her into this damaged woman that she's become?

And despite everything, being here—a prisoner—is still preferable when I think about the alternative. A life spent in silent servitude to Nero Imperioli...

Or here, with his sister.

Shaking my head, I sit on the bed. She's just as bad as he is, of course. I know all about what Hades and the Styx Syndicate have done. And it's foolish to waste sympathy on my captor. Isn't it? She's given me no reason to feel anything but fear and anger.

Still…

The image of her haunted eyes lingers in my mind.

CHAPTER 8

Hadria

A FEW DAYS after I took Aurora for my own, I stand in my personal study just off the war room and watch the latest surveillance footage of Nero. He's been rampaging since I took Aurora from him. Oh, he's *furious*, seething with rage at the audacity of his long-forgotten sister's move, unnerved to have me reappear after all these years, and all of Chicago is suffering from his tantrum.

And I know he is humiliated, too. Even *he* has used Hades' services from time to time, without knowing who it was that he'd hired. I know secrets that would put a target on his back from every player in town.

And I know all of *their* secrets, too. I've been collecting them over the years, storing them up until the time presented itself. My identity was my most closely guarded secret. I wanted the revelation to be ground-shaking—and it was, by all accounts. Every criminal outfit in the city has been talking about it.

About *me*.

So the cat's out of the bag. And now it's time to skin it.

But despite my focus on business these last few days, my thoughts keep wandering back to Aurora. There's an innocence about her, a vulnerability that tugs at something deep within me, makes me want to stamp out the light in her—but can't bring myself to do it.

I switch on the internal cameras to see what she's up to. She's been here for a few days now, and she's finally starting to settle in, to become used to our ways of living at night rather than day. Mrs. Graves has been taking good care of her, and I've made sure my men keep their distance.

I watch now as she paces in her room, wandering aimlessly. She's wearing a plain gray sweatshirt, the oversized fabric swallowing her petite frame, her shorts peeking out only occasionally as she creeps along. Her long hair is loose around her shoulders, and she looks younger than her years.

I'm not sure why I'm spying on her like this.

She's a means to an end, nothing more. But there's something about her that draws me in. Maybe it's that very innocence, her naivety about the world we live in.

Or maybe it was the way she looked at me with those big, doe-like eyes, as if she saw something in me that I can't see myself, and whispered her thanks to me for saving her from Nero.

Whatever it is, I can't shake it off. I find myself watching her more and more, even when I know I should be focusing on other things.

I haven't seen her in person again since the day I took her. Something keeps me away, some instinct for danger. Because she *is* dangerous, somehow. Not like I am. No, Aurora is dangerous like a beautiful, poisonous plant, something delicate and deadly.

Deadly to me alone, perhaps.

It's late, coming on for dawn, and I know I should finish up and head to bed. But I can't tear my eyes away from the screen as Aurora paces back and forth. I'm addicted to the sight of her.

I thought once I *had* her, I'd be satisfied. She belongs to me and will always belong to me.

Why can't that knowledge be enough?

On the monitor, she suddenly looks around, as if sensing someone's presence. I hold my breath, foolishly afraid she'll see me through the camera.

But of course she doesn't. She just stands there for a moment, before she goes to the door of her quarters and pulls it open, just a crack. She presses her face to the opening and looks out at the hallway beyond for a moment. Then she closes it, turns, and continues to pace her room.

That's the farthest she's gotten since she's been here. She hasn't dared go beyond the door of her rooms, despite my telling her she could explore the house.

I exhale, yawn. I need to get a hold of myself. This obsession with her is going to be my downfall. It's time to get some sleep. Tomorrow is another day, and I have a city to take over, after all.

I leave my study and head down the hallway, my footsteps echoing in the empty corridor. As I pass by the junction that leads down to Aurora's rooms, I can't help but glance her way.

I wonder what she's dreaming about.

Over the next few days, I can't resist spying on Aurora through the security cameras whenever I'm in my study alone. But things seem to be changing, and not for the better. She rarely leaves her bed now, and when she does, all I see is the defeated slump of her shoulders. She used to radiate vibrancy, life.

Now that light seems…dimmed.

It's only been a few days but she looks thinner. Paler. Dark circles under her eyes. And this fading spirit troubles me in ways I cannot explain.

When I claimed her that day, bursting into the wedding chapel to take what was rightfully mine, she burned bright as the sun, defiant even with fear in her eyes. She was the same as a girl, too, that teenager who stared straight at me as I exited her tiny house.

Now it seems the spark in her has been smothered, extinguished by her captivity here in my stronghold.

And I shouldn't care.

But I do.

I summon Mrs. Graves, my most trusted member of staff and the one who has been tasked with tending to the girl, and I question her about Aurora, masking my concern with nonchalance. Yet anger rises in me as she reports her refusal to eat, the long hours she spends staring at nothing.

Leaning forward, I demand, "Has she been harmed under my roof?"

Mrs. Graves shows impatience that I wouldn't tolerate in any member of the Syndicate. "No, ma'am, she most certainly has not. But you can't shut a girl up in darkness and *not* expect her to fade."

I dismiss her abruptly, unsatisfied. I live my life in the night just fine, as do all my people. No, I'm sure it must be something more. So I gather the staff into my war room, and I read them the riot act. Halfway through, Lyssa slips into the room.

I bet Mrs. Graves told her to come in here. They all think Lyssa is the only one who can talk me down when I'm furious.

Well, they're not wrong.

But I ignore Lyssa for now and demand again who has been harassing Aurora—my eye happens to fall on one of the kitchen hands as I ask, and he goes pale.

"No one's hurt her, ma'am, I swear it," he stammers.

"If a single hair on her head is harmed, you'll lose your whole scalp. She is under my protection." My ice-cold glare dares him to defy me, but he just shakes his head vigorously.

The rest of them continue to glance between each other, confused. "We haven't touched her, ma'am," offers Angie, the only other housemaid allowed to give Aurora personal service. "I try to be kind when I go in with her meals. But she just sits there, won't eat a thing we bring her. And she…she gets these fits sometimes, crying and pacing like a caged animal."

Aurora in tears? Aurora fading away like a neglected house plant?

I search their faces for deceit. I find none.

Lyssa intervenes. "Hadria, for God's sake," she says, strolling up toward me. "The girl's been treated fairly. She's warm, well-fed, and safe as a baby in its crib." She drops her voice as she comes closer. "Can't expect to shut up a sunbeam in a box and not have it dim a little. Hm?"

I exhale slowly, then give an irritated flick of my hand. "Get out of here, all of you." I glare at Lyssa so that she knows she's included in that command, but all she does is smirk as though it amuses her. But she leaves the room with the rest.

Lyssa is right, though I won't admit it. Did I really expect to cage the light within this girl and not have her fade a little?

But what does it matter, after all? She's mine now. That's all that matters.

Yet somehow the thought of her radiance fading fills me with an emotion I can't quite place. Something…

Something close to what I imagine sorrow must feel like.

I knew claiming her would provoke chaos, force Nero's hand. I planned on it. In that sense, it's been a satisfactory outcome, but this unforeseen complication is clouding my victory, this strange protectiveness, this inconvenient attraction I feel for her.

Attraction? I'm not sure that's the word. Whatever this is, it runs deeper, speaks to something more primal within me. All I know is that I can't bear to see that fragile light wane, its warmth and comfort leeched away by the cold pragmatism that rules Elysium.

And so, before I can talk myself out of it, I go to her room and fling open the door. Startled, she jerks up in bed. But aside from that, she doesn't cry out, doesn't react.

I sit on the end of the bed and meet her eyes, keeping my voice even. "You need to eat."

She simply stares at her hands, her cuticles ragged where she's been picking at them.

I try again, using the same voice I use on my soldiers. "Did you hear me, Aurora? You will eat when you are presented with food."

For the first time she meets my gaze. Her voice is a ragged whisper. "Please let me go. Please. I don't belong here."

My heart constricts.

I wasn't aware I still had one.

"Would you rather I returned you to my brother?" I ask her coldly. "You will eat when you are brought food, or you will only have yourself to blame when I have you force-fed like a turkey being fattened up for Thanksgiving."

I sweep out of the room without waiting to see her response.

CHAPTER 9

Aurora

THE NIGHT—DAY?—AFTER Hadria told me I had to eat, I stir from restless dreams. I blink up at the ceiling, that familiar heaviness settling into my bones. I don't even know if it's day or night outside. And all I feel is fatigue. Getting up takes so much effort. Eating takes effort. Even showering feels like trying to move mountains, so I've taken to skipping it more often than not.

Sleep has become my only respite, my escape from Hadria's grasp.

Though even in my dreams, I still have my choices taken away from me.

A knock at the door jolts me from my melancholy reverie. Before I can respond, Mrs. Graves bustles in, clucking her tongue at the sight of me still in bed.

"Come now, up you get," she says briskly.

"I'm tired," I mumble into the pillows, but Mrs. Graves will have none of it. She tuts, leaning over to give my shoulder a shake.

"Lying about won't do you any good. You need a nice hot shower to perk you up."

I shrug off her touch, burrowing deeper under the covers. "Leave me alone." I was polite at first to Mrs. Graves, because she's been kind to me, but I'm too tired to bother being polite today.

The mattress dips as Mrs. Graves takes a seat. Her voice softens, threaded with concern. "Aurora, you must stop this fretting. Hadria wants you to join her for dinner tonight. So we need to have you looking presentable."

A shiver dances down my spine at the mention of Hadria. Ever since her threat to force-feed me if I didn't start taking care of myself, fear and defiance have warred within me. The thought of those cold hands touching me, holding me down...

I shake my head sharply. "I don't care what Hadria wants. I'm not some doll to be dressed up and paraded around."

Mrs. Graves' eyes gentle with sympathy. "I know this is diffi-cult, but you'll only make things worse by fighting her at every turn. Hadria rewards cooperation handsomely, believe me. And you have nothing to fear from her...as long as you obey her." When I make no move to leave the bed, her expression grows stern. "If you insist on behaving like a stubborn child, I'll have to bring Lyssa in to handle you. I doubt you want that."

My stomach lurches. I've learned a little over the time I've been here, asking a few questions of Mrs. Graves and the other maid who comes in sometimes, Angie. Lyssa is Hadria's enforcer, head of security at Elysium, and right-hand woman. Dealing with her is the last thing I want. Lyssa takes too much pleasure in needling me.

So with a grudging sigh, I throw back the covers. "Fine. I'll shower."

Mrs. Graves smiles approvingly, leading me into the opulent bathroom. I stand stiffly as she turns on the shower, gesturing for me to undress and step in. Heat rises in my cheeks.

"I'd prefer privacy, if you don't mind."

"Come on, no need to be shy." At my mulish look, she adds,

"The longer you drag your feet, the more likely Lyssa will come knocking."

I reluctantly strip off the oversized nightshirt. Goosebumps prickle my bare skin as I step under the hot spray, the water sluicing away days of built-up grime. I have to admit, it does feel soothing, warming my chilled bones.

Mrs. Graves passes me a scented body wash and urges, "Wash your hair too, that's a good girl."

I grit my teeth at being addressed like a child, but hold my tongue. There are worse battles to be fought than this. As I work up a lather in my hair, my mind inevitably wanders back to Hadria's dinner invitation.

Why summon me now, after a week without a glimpse of her? Does she mean to threaten me into better behavior? The not-knowing sits like a stone in my gut.

By the time I turn off the faucets, the mirrors are fogged with steam. Mrs. Graves wraps me in plush towels and sits me down at the vanity to gently work a comb through my wet tangles. The repetitive motion lulls me into complacency.

"What is she like?" I ask abruptly. "Under that coldness, I mean." From what little I've gleaned about the staff here, many have been in Hadria's service for years. Mrs. Graves especially seems familiar with her mistress's moods.

The older woman's eyes grow distant, a sad smile playing about her lips. "Colder still, I think. But Hadria has always been...complex. Brilliant, ambitious, but very closed off. But she is capable of great loyalty. She would do anything for the people she trusts."

I digest her words as she sets about drying my hair and curling it. It takes ages, so that I'm almost asleep again by the time she's done. Rising briskly, Mrs. Graves gives me a little shake. "Now then, let's get you dressed. Angie brought in a gown the mistress wants you to wear."

Curiosity wrestles with dread as I follow her into the

bedroom. A breathtaking dress lies draped across the bedspread, all warm sunset hues and diaphanous layers. Mrs. Graves helps me into it, cinching the corseted bodice. The skirt falls to my ankles floor in a frothy cascade of handkerchief hems.

I study my reflection and the hysterical urge to laugh bubbles up. Hadria has dressed me in shades of sunrise—ironic for a woman who prefers to live in an endless night.

"You look lovely, my dear," Mrs. Graves pronounces. Before I can form a reply, a knock sounds at the door.

My pulse kicks up when Lyssa stalks in, raking her gaze over me. "Well, well, sleeping beauty awakes. Time's wasting, Suzy. Hadria wants you downstairs."

I stand woodenly, smoothing my skirt with shaking fingers. Lyssa grasps my elbow in an iron grip, leading me down the hallway. My legs turn to jelly as we descend the floating glass stairs, partly because it makes me dizzy to look through the stairs I'm supposed to be stepping on, and partly because I'm worried about Hadria. What does she have in store?

Lyssa marches me across the foyer's smooth floor towards the closed double doors of the formal dining room. She pauses, leaning in with a smirk.

"Word of advice? Don't keep her waiting, or that pretty dress might end up stained red." She drags a crimson fingernail across my throat in emphasis.

I flinch, anger simmering beneath my fear. Gathering my courage, I push past her and throw open the doors myself.

Whatever awaits beyond them, I'll meet it on my own terms.

CHAPTER 10
Hadria

AURORA PRACTICALLY STORMS into the dining room, her eyes wide and her breath coming quick and shallow. She's dressed in the gown I chose for her, and despite the gentle colors of dawn she rather reminds me of a flame, quick and fearless, as the light fabric whirls around her like liquid fire. Her hair is a mass of shiny ringlets, flowing around that beautiful face of hers, adding to her air of vulnerability.

And she is still pale, the hollows of her cheeks more pronounced. She might remind me of a flame, but she's burning low.

I extend my hand to her, my fingers tingling slightly as she takes it and I lead her to the table. "Thank you for coming to dinner."

Her chin goes up. "Did I have a choice?"

The vibrant girl I remember might be missing, but she still has that strange fearlessness. But I don't respond to her barb. I just clear my throat and gesture to the table, which she approaches silently, her eyes running over the feast before her.

"Sit."

She sits.

"Eat."

But she does not eat.

This annoys me. I wanted this dinner to go perfectly. I wanted this silly girl to be obedient, to realize that of the fates she could have suffered, this one is the best of the lot. I pile up a plate of food and slam it down in front of her, making her jump.

And immediately I regret taking such a harsh approach. I sit back down and reconsider.

"Aurora," I say, softening my tone. "Why don't you tell me about yourself?"

She looks at me warily. "For one thing, I'm a vegetarian," she says at last.

I survey the vast spread of meat dishes laid out before us and can't help but laugh.

Aurora smiles a little, too.

I call for staff to clear away everything that is not suitable for a vegetarian. Then I carefully re-serve Aurora a new plate piled high with greens, roasted vegetables, and pasta. "There," I say, setting it gently before her. "Now *eat*. And tell me more about yourself."

I want to know her better so that I can help her understand her place here. Lyssa is better at this kind of thing than I am; I'm not exactly a people person. But I've picked up a few skills from my best friend over the years.

Aurora finally picks up her fork and starts eating. Score one to Hadria, at least.

But the awkward silence remains between us. "There's nothing much to tell," she says after a few mouthfuls.

And I'm not accustomed to dining with others, let alone making small talk.

"Well…" I begin, cursing myself for the ineloquent start. "What are your interests?"

She looks up, surprise flickering across her face. "Oh, I…" she begins hesitantly. "I like gardening."

I can't help a small snort. "*Plants* are your passion?"

Her eyes flash, but with animation rather than anger. "I love tending to living things, watching them grow. And they give us so much—food, oxygen…"

Her enthusiasm is catching. I couldn't care less about gardening, but I find myself drawn in. And underneath the shy exterior is that bright spirit I remember.

And then she goes and ruins everything.

"That's why I wanted to ask you again," she says, "if I could go outside. Into the gardens. Even once a week…"

She trails off as I raise an eyebrow. But I consider her request. My first instinct is refusal, of course. I can't risk her trying to escape into the woods that border the estate. But something in her pleading eyes stops me giving an instant *No*.

"The gardens," I repeat, keeping my voice neutral. "You want to spend time among the flowers and trees?"

She nods, a spark of hope lighting her face. "Yes. Being outside, in nature…it always made me happy before." Her voice drops as she nods to the shuttered window. "And I just know it would be nicer than being stuck inside my room all day—or night, I guess."

I bristle slightly at the critique of her quarters. But she's right. Compared to the freedom of the outdoors, I suppose it must feel dreary.

Aurora is no creature of the darkness. She was meant for open skies and fresh air, not concrete and iron. If granting her a small freedom keeps her spirits from fading, it's a reasonable compromise, surely?

But one I may come to regret, if she exploits it.

"No," I tell her. "I cannot allow it."

"But—"

"*No*," I snarl again, with more force than necessary—but I am unused to having to repeat myself.

But as I see Aurora flinch, something unpleasant washes

over me. I'm not used to having to control my temper around others; I rarely lose it in the first place. Irrationality is a liability in my world. But seeing Aurora cower from me awakens an unfamiliar feeling.

Shame.

I steady myself before I speak again. "The risk is too great during the day. But..." I hesitate, hating to make this concession. "But if some time in the gardens at night will lift your spirits, I suppose I'll permit it. You'll have Lyssa or one of my other people as an escort, of course."

Aurora's face transforms with joy and gratitude, as if I've given her the moon itself, and she reaches over to grab my hand. "Thank you, Hadria. Truly."

I let her squeeze my fingers for a moment before tugging free and brushing off her gratitude. "It's nothing. Just mind you don't track dirt inside."

Still, something warm stirs in my chest at being able to grant this small comfort to her.

"The perimeter fence is electrified," I tell her as I go back to my meal. "I would advise against testing its voltage."

Her smile fades. Good.

She must understand this is not a game.

CHAPTER 11

Aurora

UP UNTIL NOW, this dinner with Hadria was not what I was expecting. But her unspoken threat about the electric fence brings me back down to earth with a bump.

"What's going to happen to me?" I finally ask her.

Hadria regards me coolly over the rim of her wine glass. "You already know that. You'll remain here, in my home. It will be your home, too, like it is for everyone else here."

Are all those staff members prisoners too? I want to ask. But I already know the answer to that. They come and go as they please. Some of them do live here on the grounds of the estate— Mrs. Graves, for one—but even then, they can go outside and walk in the gardens.

But I'm to be kept in darkness forever, shut up in this strange house that feels more suffocating with every passing second.

"And...for how long?" It's the question I've been dreading to ask.

Hadria sets down her glass now. She leans forward, regarding me intently. "Understand this, Aurora—you *belong* to me. Your life is mine. And I won't ever let you go. It's best that you get used to the idea as soon as possible and stop sulking, like you have been."

I open my mouth in outrage to protest but she silences me with a raised hand.

"However," she continues, "I won't be cruel to you, not like my brother would have been. You'll want for nothing here. I'm not a monster—or at least, not the same breed as my brother."

Not a monster? What else could you call someone who intends to hold me captive for the rest of my life?

Sensing my defiance, Hadria's eyes harden. "You will obey the rules I've set. Attempts to contact the outside world or escape will be punished. But if you cooperate, you'll find your time here can be very comfortable. Even happy. And I want you to be happy, Aurora. You're much more pleasant when you are."

I clench my fists in my lap, trembling. I want to scream at her that she can keep me here, locked up, even keep me out of the sunlight if she likes—but she can't *make* me be happy just because it suits her.

Hadria leans back, regarding me with a hint of amusement. "Really, there's no need for such distress. You've never truly been free, anyway. Your father's been using you as a bargaining chip your whole life. As far as fates go, yours could have been *much* worse."

Her words hit hard enough to make me rear back in my chair. Because as much as I hate to admit it...

She's right.

I've been a pawn since I was a child. *My* dreams were never important. I barely dared to look ahead to the future, because I knew—from an early age—that it would be bleak. I never even bothered to think about what kind of life I wanted to make for myself, because I knew...

I knew I never would.

And now I never will.

I slump down, defeated. What chance do I have against

someone like Hades? For now, it seems I have no choice but to accept my fate.

But I swear to myself, someday I *will* take my freedom. Hadria might think she owns me, but she doesn't own my spirit.

Mrs. Graves said that Hadria would do anything for the people she trusted. So even if it takes me years to earn Hadria's trust, I will. I'll get her to trust me enough to slacken off on her restrictions. And then I'll take an opportunity to escape, to get out of here, out of the city, the *country*. For now, I'll bide my time, play her game.

And one day, I swear it, I'll be free.

───────

I've become grudgingly accustomed to the topsy-turvy lifestyle here at Elysium, but my forays into the garden each night still make me feel strangely adrift. The moon and starlight casts everything in an ethereal glow, emphasizing how far away I am from everything that was once familiar.

Tonight, a few nights after Hadria granted me permission to go into the grounds, I'm exploring west of the house. The estate is enormous enough that I fear getting lost—especially at night—so that I haven't ventured all that far away from the house, yet.

Even though I know I'm always under watch. The first night it was Lyssa, who I asked to hang back a little, at least let me pretend I was alone.

She did, after a deeply sarcastic comment. And since then, I've been allowed out to wander wherever I like, which means that someone, somewhere, is following me without my knowledge. But I appreciate the illusion of solitude, at least.

Not enough to thank Lyssa, though, since I know it must be her orders that keep the spies at a distance.

I run my fingers over the leaves of an olive tree, inhaling the earthy scent of the recently-turned flower beds nearby. The grounds are my only refuge in Hadria's busy fortress. Elysium is alive at night and dead during the day. In the darkness the estate thrives; there are comings and goings of Styx Syndicate members, and visits from people that it took me a few nights to realize were emissaries from other criminal groups, stern-looking men in dark suits arriving in sleek cars. Always here for meetings with Hadria in that war room of hers.

I've begun to glimpse a world of secrets, of transactions made in the dead of night. And I've started to identify her inner circle.

Lyssa, with her wild blonde hair and unnerving smile, is Hadria's most trusted lieutenant. She takes a perverse delight in taunting me whenever our paths cross. "Enjoying yourself, Suzy Sunshine?" she'll ask with a smirk. I say nothing, unwilling to show weakness, but the truth is, Lyssa scares me as much as Hadria—more, maybe, since Lyssa seems to lack the same self-control that makes Hadria so perfectly poised and ice-cold.

The man with the missing fingers, the one who carried me from the car to the steps of the house on the first day I arrived, is another of Hadria's lieutenants. I think he's called Ricky Half-hands, though that seems cruel to me. He's guarded but polite if he ever happens to catch sight of me, giving me a gentlemanly nod. I like him more than a guy I've heard called "the Taxman," who I thought at first must have been an accountant. But he's one of Hadria's senior mercenaries as well, it turns out, and I try to avoid him. He looks at me so coldly, not like Hadria, but as though I'm an object of interest kept in a glass case. Something valuable…but still an object.

The last of Hadria's inner circle is another woman, an ice-blonde who speaks with an accent—Russian, maybe? Definitely Eastern European. I don't know her name, but most of the time I see her, her clothes are stained with blood.

So I guess she's effective at what she does.

Others around the mansion treat me with caution, as if I'm a bomb that could detonate at any moment. Hadria's hulking house guards watch me with suspicion. Angie, the maid who sometimes turns over my room, offers me tentative smiles and speaks kindly to me, but always shuts down any conversation beyond small talk. Other staff members sort of absent themselves as soon as I walk into a room, so that I'm starting to feel invisible sometimes.

And Mrs. Graves is somehow simultaneously motherly but distant, and most of the time when I ask questions, she goes conveniently deaf.

But these uneasy dynamics with everyone reveal Hadria's absolute authority. No one dares overstep her rules regarding me. Hadria oversees this empire with an iron fist, commanding…and feared.

But I can see, too, that she's loved by some. Loved by Lyssa, certainly, with a fierce loyalty that surprised me at first. Mrs. Graves speaks of Hadria with deep affection and, sometimes, reverence. Maybe it's not so surprising. My own feelings about Hadria remain complicated, after all. Unease grips me when I'm in her presence. But a traitorous fascination still lurks beneath the surface.

I'm drawn to her strength, her self-possession. She moves through this world with purpose…

Unlike me.

When she first shut me up in here, I was certain she would hurt me. But apart from my confinement, she has done nothing bad to me. I barely see her, in fact. The dinner was the last time I was in her presence alone. Since then, she's stopped by only once or twice to inquire after my health—exactly like that, formally inquiring after my health—and only when Angie or Mrs. Graves are there.

I might cling to the hope that she'll release me someday, or that I'll find a way to freedom, but Hadria seems content to keep me for now. She's collected me, almost, like one of the weird modern art paintings and sculptures dotted around the place.

And in the meantime, I've become nocturnal, like everyone else under her rule, and I wander the moonlit gardens like a ghost.

Tonight I'm heading back to a forgotten corner that I came across a few nights ago—a night garden that nature had begun to reclaim. I've heard them called night gardens, moon gardens, dark gardens; all titles seem appropriate to me. The plants here only bloom at night, and many of them are a glowing white color under the moonlight. But it's been sadly neglected and I've been clearing it out a little, trying to coax it back to life.

It gives me something to do, if nothing else, and the moon is bright enough tonight that I can see quite well. Kneeling beside a tangle of vines, I gently free a struggling rose bush from a thorny circle of weeds. After that, I move slowly through the garden, tending to more plants in turn.

As I reach the center of the night garden, I pause at the moon dial, tracing its silvered face. This place of neglect could become a little sanctuary for me, one space I can shape as I please. Hadria will never know about it, after all. She's supremely uninterested in the grounds—and in me, it seems.

And I should be happy about that, I remind myself. You don't *want* some vicious mercenary taking an interest in you. My interest in her—more than that, I can admit it now: my childish crush on her—seems so silly now. Now that I understand what it really means to belong to her.

But out in the night garden, I *almost* feel a sense of freedom. Surrounded by nature, I can forget about my prison and connect to something true. For a few blessed hours each night, maybe I can simply *be*.

I rarely think of the outside world anymore. What use is it? I certainly don't think of my father, and I'm still relieved I was stolen away from Nero. My mother…yes. I do think of her sometimes.

But what I truly want is more abstract than people or places. I just want to be *free*. The more the days pass, the more I want what I have never had: the freedom to come and go as I please. To make my own choices—my own mistakes.

Instead, I spend my time tending the night garden and, when I tire of that, I haunt the front of the mansion, slipping among the hedges and stone walls, watching the people come and go.

Watching.

Wondering.

Waiting.

Until at last one night, when dawn is approaching and I know I have to get back into my cage before the sun rises, I make my weary way back to my bedroom and stop dead in the doorway.

Hadria is in my room.

Hadria is sitting on my bed, leaning up against the cushions, clad only in a black silk robe, and as I watch, she uncrosses her ankles and the silk slides off her perfect white thigh.

My mouth goes dry.

I quickly avert my eyes. "H-Hadria. I wasn't expecting you."

She regards me with those silvery eyes, almost like liquid moonlight. "No," she says. "Did you enjoy your time in the gardens?"

I nod mutely.

"Come here." Her voice brooks no argument. I approach cautiously and perch on the edge of the mattress beside her. Hadria studies me for a moment before speaking again.

"Your mother has been…persistent in requesting a visitation. Rather a nuisance, in fact."

My eyes widen in surprise. I haven't seen or spoken to my mother since Hadria stole me away on my wedding day. The thought of being reunited with her, even briefly, makes my heart ache.

Hadria continues, "I've decided to grant her request to see you, provided you wish to see her as well."

I'm shocked by Hadria's uncharacteristic leniency. She seems to read the question in my expression.

"Consider it a show of good faith between us," she says quietly. "I know your time here has been difficult. But when I said I wanted you to be happy, Aurora, I meant it."

I'm touched by this glimpse of consideration behind Hadria's usual cold facade. "Thank you," I manage to get out. "I *would* like to see my mother again."

Hadria nods. "I'll arrange it then. But Aurora..." Her eyes harden. "Do not mistake my generosity for weakness. You are still mine, and you will always remain here in Elysium."

The tender moment evaporates. I drop my gaze, the familiar weight of captivity pressing down on me again.

"Of course, Hadria."

I feel her eyes on me for a long moment, and then she stands and sweeps out of the room without another word, the silk robe whispering behind her. I fall onto the pillows she lay against just moments ago, my mind spinning, and breathe in her scent— alluring, mysterious, sharp...

Just like the woman herself.

CHAPTER 12

Hadria

"HAVE you completely lost your mind, you silly bitch?" Lyssa snaps.

I suck in a breath between my teeth as I let my temper rise and fade. "Have *you* lost your desire to live? If anyone else spoke to me like that—"

"Yes, yes; you'd flay them alive," Lyssa says impatiently. "But when you tell me you're having a *dinner party* for your captive and her mommy dearest, what do you expect me to say?"

We're in the war room, alone—which is lucky for Lyssa, because if she spoke to me like that in front of anyone, I'd backhand her at once—and she has her hands on her hips and an exasperated expression on her face.

"The mother has been incessant in her demands," I tell her.

"So fucking what?" Lyssa explodes, throwing her hands up. "You're *Hades*. Cut her goddamn tongue out and send it to that husband of hers as a fresh warning. He's the one you should be worried about, since he's buddied up to Nero."

In the weeks since I abducted his bride, Nero has been trying to amass an army. Unfortunately for him, he's not well liked, and there are not many in Chicago who are interested in going up against the legendary Hades, not without a guaranteed win.

They know what will happen to them otherwise.

But Aurora's father still owes Nero a huge sum of money—the sum that Aurora was supposed to be payment for—and so his life is now forfeit until Aurora is returned to Nero.

Which she never will be.

"I don't give the slightest fuck *what* Aurora's father is doing," I tell Lyssa. "He's a sniveling little fool and—"

"And he's got poker buddies in high places."

With a sigh, I have to admit that she's right about that. I had wondered myself what was keeping a nonentity like Jimmy Verderosa alive all these years, given the size and number of his debts. The answer was his connections—not in the underworld, but the righteous world. He's friendly with judges and police chiefs, the kind of people who can be very useful to someone like Nero.

And very irritating to a business like mine.

"The father has not been invited to this dinner," I tell Lyssa. "Just her mother. And you can't imagine *she'll* come here with any weapon but tears."

Lyssa gives me a look that tells me she still thinks I'm crazy, but she says no more about it as some of the senior Syndicate members begin to file in for our meeting tonight.

And I turn my mind to business—and to reclaiming my birthright.

A day later, I stand outside Aurora's bedroom door, steeling myself before I knock. She's been here at Elysium for over three weeks now, and in that time, I've kept my distance. Watching her from afar, ensuring her safety and comfort from the shadows. I allow myself to check the cameras only three times a day, because otherwise they're too great a distraction.

But tonight I will see her face to face again, and I'm not sure why I'm so hesitant.

I knock at last, and a muffled voice bids me enter. Aurora sits at her vanity, brushing out her long hair, wearing a fluffy shell-pink robe. She must have just come out of her shower. I'm relieved she's washing regularly now, and eating, too, though she's still paler than I'd like. Our eyes meet in the mirror, and she turns, surprise flashing across her delicate features.

"Hadria?"

My name on her lips sends a thrill through me. I incline my head in greeting and close the door behind me.

"I've come to escort you to dinner."

Aurora frowns, glancing at the clock, which reads just before five p.m. "Do you mean breakfast? I usually have it brought up. Besides, isn't it early…so to speak?"

She's adjusted well to Elysium's schedule by now. I fold my hands behind my back, affecting nonchalance. "I meant a traditional dinner in this case. We have a guest arriving shortly to share it with us. Your mother."

At this, Aurora stands swiftly, her brush clattering to the floor. "My mother is coming here?"

The naked hope in her voice twists something in my chest. This girl has been starved of kindness in her life. And it's a quality I discarded long ago.

"I told you I would permit her a visit. I extended an invitation for tonight, so she can see for herself that you're unharmed." I keep my tone neutral and watch Aurora closely. "I thought a dinner would be most suitable."

Her eyes glisten with tears, but she blinks them back. Chin lifting, she meets my gaze directly. "Thank you, Hadria."

The simple words undo me, and I turn away, clearing my throat. "Yes, well, she'll be arriving in an hour or so, so you should come down to the foyer around six. Wear that white thing I had sent in yesterday."

I want her in white. I like the virginal innocence it suggests. It helps keep my darker desires tamped down when I remind myself that Aurora is still untouched.

She gives a little smile. "I'll be there—if I can find the way. I still get a little lost sometimes. I have a terrible sense of direction."

"Then I'll fetch you," I say at once, "and escort you down. It would be fitting, after all."

She stares at me for a long moment, and I think her cheeks look a little pinker. "Alright," she says softly. "Thank you."

At six on the dot, I go back to her room and knock again. She opens the door with a genuine smile, and I can see now how unhappy she really has been here, until tonight.

And she's undeniably beautiful, even in a simple white shift, her hair pulled back in a low ponytail from a face that is difficult to pull my eyes away from. "I'm ready," she says with excitement. "Is she here?"

"She will be soon." I offer my hand, and she takes it, even squeezes my fingers happily. Side by side, we walk through the house until we get to the floating glass staircase that leads down into the foyer. But voices already echo up from the foyer—Sylvia Verderosa has arrived, just this moment it seems. Mrs. Graves is greeting her at the door, though I hear a questioning note in her voice.

And then Sylvia steps aside and the reason for Mrs. Graves' reluctance becomes clear as Aurora's father slinks into view.

Next to me, Aurora stifles a gasp and recoils, clutching at my arm like a lifeline.

And rage surges within me, white-hot and visceral. How dare this cretin come here, after all he has done to her?

They haven't noticed us yet, observing them from the landing. I turn, grasping Aurora's shoulders firmly until her frightened gaze meets mine. "Aurora. Do you want them to leave?" My voice is steel sheathed in silk.

She hesitates, lips trembling. I force myself to remain still, letting her decide. Finally, she whispers, "I think I'll be okay if... if you stay close."

I nod, a silent vow, before guiding her down the steps. Sylvia rushes forward with a cry, enfolding Aurora in her arms. Aurora clings to her mother, tears flowing freely now. But I stand guard, blocking her father's path when he attempts to approach.

"She's not yours to touch," I tell him. Sullen, he steps back. "I'm surprised you had the nerve to show up here, Verderosa. Or perhaps you're just that stupid."

"She's my daughter, too!" he blusters, and then grows nervous at my cool stare. "I mean...if you don't mind...Sylvia said there was a dinner..."

"As a sign of my mercy, I'll allow you to stay," I tell him at last, when I've judged he's squirmed *just* enough. "But this is the last time you'll benefit from my goodwill." Aurora hasn't even heard him, at least; she's too busy answering her mother's tearful flow of questions.

I allow mother and daughter a moment more before interrupting. "Shall we adjourn to the dining room?"

Throughout the meal I keep Aurora's father firmly in my sights, interceding whenever he addresses her directly.

And under the table, Aurora's knee presses against mine like a touchstone.

And then I steer the conversation toward business, heedless of Aurora's father's protestations. I ask him how much it would take for him to see sense and turn informer on Nero for me.

"You can hardly expect…anyway, that's enough of that," he says with a weak chuckle. "The women shouldn't be bothered with such things." He indicates Sylvia and Aurora.

"The women? I *am* a woman. And as this is my table, my food, and my…" I trail off, meeting Aurora's eyes briefly. "…my *guest*, I will choose when and where to discuss business." Aurora's father shrinks under my gaze, but she's watching me closely as I continue. "In fact, I believe it's high time Aurora learned the full truth about her father." Ignoring his sputtering, I turn to Aurora and begin laying out the finer points of her father's criminal dealings.

He's not like me, of course. He's no killer, not even a made man. But he's taken part in enough thefts, swindles and embezzlements that he'd be put away for quite some time—if he didn't have the friends that he does. And he must have dirt on them, too, because no one could like this little toad for his personality.

And those secrets give him power over these so-called friends.

Aurora listens raptly. I can see the exact moment the veil lifts from her eyes. She begins to comprehend, perhaps for the first time, the true depth of her father's dishonor. The conversation continues, but Aurora does not waver. She absorbs the ugliest of realities without flinching.

And my respect for her strengthens.

Her mother just sits there, staring at her plate. Sylvia's either heard all this before or she suspected it already.

Halfway through dessert, my head bodyguard comes in and speaks softly in my ear. "A group of petitioners from the Sokolov *bratva*, Hades."

"Send them up," I say.

Artie's not dumb enough to contradict me, but he does hesitate for a split-second.

"Send them up," I tell him again, nodding so that he knows I understand his reticence. If only he realized how convenient this visit is.

I need to blow off a little steam.

"Yes, Hades," he says, and a few minutes later, a commotion sounds from the drive. Gravel scatters beneath squealing tires, and car doors slam.

I already know what this is about. A week ago, one faction of the Sokolov *bratva* asked the Syndicate to deal with another faction. We did—and they didn't pay up.

So yesterday, I sent some of my people to deal with the matter: they killed one of the original faction's men. A low-level soldier, but a warning nonetheless.

And yet somehow, I don't think they're here tonight with their tails between their legs and the money they owe me.

Excusing myself with a nod, I leave Aurora and her parents under the eyes of two house guards and I go out myself to the front steps just as four men spill from two vehicles.

Their leader sneers. "Hey, sweetheart. We have a message from our Boss."

How predictable they are.

Ever since I revealed myself as not just a woman working for Hades, but Hades himself, some of the men in this city's underworld have had difficulty coming to terms with my sex. I expected it. Even hoped for it. And it happening here tonight is perfect timing, because I am full of pent-up irritation from letting Jimmy Verderosa sit at my table and eat my food.

I descend slowly, savoring the looks of dawning wariness on their faces. "A message?" My voice rings out, deceptively calm. Inside, I'm alive with coursing danger. With purpose. "Then give it to me."

They all glance at each other, and the leader gives a nod to one of them, who springs into action. But when he rushes at me, I slide around his blow, catching his wrist and using his momentum to throw him headfirst into the stone balustrade next to me. The noise of his skull crunching makes the others hesitate.

Their mistake.

I close the distance to the next nearest in two steps, disarming him with a vicious elbow to the temple. The knife he held falls into my hand instead, and I slide it into his neck, smooth as warm butter, then slip behind their so-called leader, pressing the blade to his throat just firmly enough to draw a thin line of blood. He freezes, watching his compatriot bleed out, choking, next to him.

"I'd really enjoy killing all of you. But I *just* had the driveway washed down from the viscera of the last fools who tried this." That's quite true. A pack of Sokolovs turned up like this just two nights ago, looking for payback for the original killings. Unfortunately for them, Lyssa happened to be the one who came to the door instead of me. "So go and tell your master to come to the dance himself next time, because I'd be delighted to separate him from his cock. Now get out of here, before I change my mind about letting you live."

I release the man with a shove, sending him stumbling into his surviving brother's arms. They each scramble into a car and speed away, tires fishtailing in their haste.

I mount the steps once more, and hand the knife to one of my house guards. A single crimson drop stains the cuff of my white shirt. Ah, well. Mrs. Graves does like a laundry challenge.

"Clean that up," I tell the door guards, thumbing over my shoulder at the bodies, and they jump to obey.

Inside, Aurora and her parents have come into the foyer, and for a moment I'm sorry that they seem to have witnessed it, since the front doors were open. Jimmy and Sylvia are dumbstruck. But Aurora…

As I approach, her expression looks something like awe.

Seizing the moment, I step close, pitching my voice low so

only she can hear. "In my world, power is the only language that is understood. Remember that, Aurora."

She blinks those fathomless eyes up at me, and I know my message was received and understood.

Turning briskly, I address her parents. "An unfortunate ending to our evening, but perhaps it's time for you to take your leave." To Sylvia, I soften my tone. "You may return soon, with proper notice. But he—" I point a finger at Aurora's father without looking his way "—will not set foot on my territory again, unless he wishes to lose his life."

After their departure—silent, fearful—I turn to Aurora again. She showed courage tonight, but now she sways on her feet, emotionally exhausted. "I'm sorry if tonight was difficult for you."

After a moment, she says, "It was. But I think...I think it was necessary, too." She regards me for a moment, a tiny crease between her brows. "Thank you, Hadria. For opening up my eyes."

"Go to your room, Sunshine. I can't have you out in the gardens tonight, not if enemies are milling around."

Mutely, she nods and makes her way up the great staircase, disappearing off to her wing of the house. Only then do I blow out a long sigh, rolling my neck to relieve the tension there.

Much occurred tonight that requires reflection. And I think best in my war room, seated on that chair my people like to call my throne. So I make my way there, and I sink into the high-backed leather chair at the head of the room. Then, since no one is here, I sling one leg up over one of the arms, slouching down, and let my chin rest in my hand.

And I begin to think.

My introspection is interrupted by the quiet creak of the door ten minutes later. I glance up to see Aurora's too-familiar silhouette against the light.

I raise my voice to say, "I told you to go to your room."

She continues forward. "I know. But there's something I want to do first."

I straighten in my chair as she draws near, wary as always when any other human being is so close to me. But she only sinks to her knees before me, her white skirts pooling on the floor around her, and bows her head in a supplicant, submissive pose.

The sight steals my breath.

"You said you wanted me to be happy," she begins.

"I do."

"Then I'd like to make a request."

I master myself with effort. "You may ask, but I make no promises."

Aurora's lips curve in a faint smile as she looks up at me. "That's fair. What I ask is this: teach me to defend myself. Teach me to be strong…like you."

I search her upturned face, wondering what this is about.

"Tonight was an education," Aurora continues when I don't immediately respond. "And during my time here I've begun to see that there are ugly truths I never wanted to face. But if I'm to live in your world, I *do* need to face those truths, need to learn how to deal with danger. And I…I need to change, if I'm going to survive here."

Still I stay silent. I have no idea what to say to her.

"You told me just before that power is the only true language in your world," she goes on at last, a faint plea in her voice. "So teach me your language, Hadria. Make me strong enough that no one can ever use me as a pawn again. Let me have some tiny measure of power in myself, since I…I know now that I'll always belong to you."

Emotion swells within me, unfamiliar yet not unwelcome. This clever little thing has seen the truth in a way few ever have. And it would be a sin to deny her growth.

I stand and take the two steps down off the dais, then hold

out a hand to her. "Very well." She takes my hand, and I draw her up to stand before me. "But first, you'll need to prove to me that you can follow orders. So tomorrow we'll begin your instruction. Meet me here in the war room an hour after breakfast."

The answering smile Aurora bestows on me illuminates her from within. Impulsively, I brush a stray strand of hair from her cheek.

"Thank you, Hadria," she breathes.

Something inside me cracks a little. Melts. "Go to bed," I tell her, pulling back. "And rest up. Because tomorrow I intend to put you through your paces."

Lyssa is going to be furious with me.

Again.

CHAPTER 13

Aurora

AT THE APPOINTED TIME, I make my way down the long hallway toward Hadria's war room. As I get closer, I hear Lyssa's raised voice coming from the open doors.

"—crazy, even for you! Giving a prisoner a weapon? You've lost your *mind* over this girl."

I freeze outside the doors, my heart pounding. Before I can decide whether to keep walking or turn back, Hadria's sharp voice slices through the air.

"Get in here, Aurora."

I jump, startled that she somehow knew I was here. Taking a deep breath, I step away from the wall and through the doorway.

The table and chairs are as they were last night, except that Lyssa stands near the head of the table, glaring at me, and Hadria is half-seated on the table itself opposite Lyssa, her posture relaxed but her light gray eyes tracking my every movement.

"Come here," Hadria orders.

I walk over obediently, though I'm acutely aware of Lyssa's

hostile stare. Hadria reaches over to Lyssa and takes a sharp dagger out of her belt before her lieutenant can react.

And then Hadria presses the hilt into my hand.

"Attack me," Hadria says calmly.

"Hadria—"

"Shut up, Lyssa. Aurora: attack me."

I stare at her, confused.

"You heard me," Hadria says. "Come at me with the knife." When I don't move, stunned by the bizarre request, her eyes harden. "Do it. Now."

I don't actually want to hurt her. But...I'm supposed to be showing her I can follow orders. So I half-heartedly lunge forward, telegraphing my movement. Hadria easily steps aside and twists my wrist, forcing me to drop the blade.

"Pathetic," she says. "Again."

Shaken, I pick up the knife and try again, putting a little more effort behind the swing this time. But Hadria again anticipates my action and disarms me with humiliating ease.

"You'd better mean it this time," Hadria says, just as cool as ever. "Stop holding back."

Anger and frustration well up inside me. I'm so tired of being at her mercy. Gripping the dagger tightly, I slash towards her with real intent, a growl escaping me.

But Hadria sidesteps my wild swing, grabbing my wrist and twisting my arm up behind my back in one smooth motion. I cry out as she slams me face down onto the table, my cheek scraping against the rough wood.

I try to struggle, but Hadria presses her body against my back, pinning me in place. Her crotch presses into my butt as she leans over me.

"Not bad," she murmurs in my ear. "But you have a lot to learn, Sunshine."

I continue to squirm, my anger fading into awareness of how vulnerable I am. Hadria's breath tickles my neck and I feel the heat of her body enveloping me. To my dismay, a traitorous shiver of arousal runs through me at her closeness.

What's wrong with me? I should despise her, not crave her touch.

Hadria releases my arm and steps back. I stand up slowly, avoiding her penetrating gaze, and rub at my cheekbone to try to hide the heat I feel spreading across my face.

"It's too dangerous," Lyssa says. She hasn't moved the whole time, and when I look at her, she practically looks *through* me instead of at me.

Hadria strides over to Lyssa and holds out a hand. "Give me your gun."

Lyssa's scowl deepens but she's too well-trained to disobey, passing over the handgun from her other hip. Hadria checks the clip, then crosses over to me. I tense, unsure of her intentions.

Without a word, she presses the gun into my palm. The metal is cold, the weight unfamiliar. Hadria walks down to the end of the room and stands straight against the wall, hands behind her back.

"Shoot me," she calls down.

My fingers curl around the grip. Is this a test? Some cruel game?

"Hadria," Lyssa snaps. "This is madness."

But Hadria ignores her, just like before. "Three shots," she says, eyes on me. "Go on. Or no more midnight gardening."

My breath hitches. I raise the gun with trembling hands. Hadria stands motionless twenty feet away, cold eyes unwavering.

I squeeze the trigger.

The gun jerks in my grip, and I'm surprised by the recoil, how hard it is on my wrists. The shot goes wild, missing Hadria by several feet. Lyssa snickers.

"Again," Hadria orders.

I steel myself and fire. The second shot echoes, even farther off target. One left.

But I've stopped shaking this time. If this is really what Hadria wants, she can damn well have it. I aim carefully at her torso and pull the trigger.

Next to her ear, the bullet thuds home, and even Hadria looks a little surprised at how close I came.

But it's still another miss. I let my hand drop, pulse racing. Hadria jogs back up and shrugs at Lyssa, amusement flickering in her eyes. "She couldn't hit water if she fell out of a boat. I think I'll be fine."

And then Hadria plucks the gun from my shaking hands. Her touch lingers, sending a shiver through me.

"And when you've trained her to take the wing off a butterfly thirty feet away?" Lyssa asks, high and cold.

Hadria gives a grim smile. "Then I'll depend on *you* to do your job and protect me. Now, Aurora and I are going to the range. I don't want to be interrupted."

She walks away without a backward glance. But I do look at Lyssa, who is still staring at me with an unreadable expression. She tilts her head slightly, then makes the unmistakable gesture of pointing her first and middle fingers at her own eyes, then pointing them straight at me.

I'm watching you.

I hurry to catch up with Hadria and then match her long steps as she leads me through the sprawling house, down to a back room on the lower floor, where she shows me a blank square sitting inconspicuously in one of the wall panels. Hadria presses her hand to it, and it comes to life: a scanner, scanning over her handprint. Then a faint click sounds and the wall panel next to me slides open to reveal a staircase descending into darkness.

I hesitate, anxiety knotting in my stomach. Hadria pauses, fixing me with an assessing look. "You have nothing to fear, Aurora," she says seriously. "On my authority, no harm will come to you at Elysium."

Her words surprise me, especially after her threats to take the gardens away from me, but hearing my name on her lips sends the same confusing thrill through me that it always does.

We descend the shadowed staircase and step out into an underground shooting range, complete with a weapons room that would rival that of a small army. My mouth drops open at this state-of-the-art facility secreted below the house.

Hadria's mouth curves slightly at my awestruck expression. "Impressive, yes? But marksmanship is a crucial skill in my line of business, as I'm sure you understand."

I swallow hard as her reference to her criminal power hangs in the air between us. It's a harsh truth, but I'm at the mercy of a dangerous woman.

"All my soldiers train here," she goes on. "And so will you."

"I've never heard anything," I say after a moment. "Any... shooting, I mean."

"Soundproofed." Hadria leads me past empty shooting stalls to a locked metal cabinet at one side. With practiced ease, she retrieves a sleek handgun, checking the clip and chamber before turning to me. "These are my own," she tells me by way of explanation. "Have you ever fired a gun before?"

I shake my head mutely.

"Then it's time you learned. Being able to defend yourself is a basic life skill, Aurora."

She's right. Enough trembling. If I want to survive, I need to adapt. "Teach me."

Without another word, she guides me into the nearest stall and hands me noise-canceling earmuffs and protective glasses. Once I have the gear in place, she shifts into instructor mode.

After a talk about the basics of gun safety that sounds almost surreal coming from *her*, she gives me the gun.

"This is a Glock 19 semi-automatic 9mm pistol. Grip it firmly in both hands like so..."

She moves behind me, guiding my hands into the proper hold on the weapon, her breath warming the nape of my neck. I repress the urge to arch into her sudden closeness. Hadria nudges my feet into position with the toe of her boot, adjusting my stance, and my own breath quickens.

"Dominant hand here, support hand here. Good. Now, look down the sight and focus on the target at the end of the stall."

I peer down the barrel at a paper outline of a human torso, black against white, hanging thirty feet away. Planting my feet, I tighten my grip and line up the sights.

"When ready, squeeze the trigger slowly. Don't yank it."

Taking a deep breath, I squeeze the trigger. The recoil punches my hands back as a shot explodes from the gun. I completely miss the target.

Hadria's hands brace me firmly. "Again. This time, expect the recoil."

I fire three more times but hit nothing except the back wall. Frustration wells up inside me. Hadria places her hand on my shoulder, voice stern.

"You're tense. Your stance is rigid. Here..."

She moves closer behind me, almost pressing against my back. Hadria's hands grasp my hips, lightly angling them sideways. One hand glides up my forearm, maneuvering my aim, while the other splays across my ribcage. Her touch sends little thrills across my skin, gentle yet commanding.

"Try it now," she murmurs, her lips near my ear.

I'm hyperaware of her body fitted to mine. *Focus*, I tell myself angrily. Blocking out the distracting sensation of Hadria's hands on me, I stare down the sight, exhaling slowly. When I squeeze the trigger this time, the shot punches through the target's right shoulder.

"Better," Hadria says. "But I want perfection. Again."

The next three shots strike the chest in a cluster. Exhilaration courses through me. I did it!

"I hit it! Did you see?" I cry out joyfully. In my excitement, I start to turn—

Hadria's hand clamps on my shoulder, holding me in place. "Don't wave around a goddamn loaded gun. Rookie mistake. And yes, I saw. But one decent grouping isn't enough. We're drilling this until you're perfect every time."

Chastened, I reset my stance. Hadria's tone is stern, almost cold. Under her critical eye, I repeat the exercise again and again until my shots consistently hit the kill zones she indicates. My hands are growing sore, but Hadria pushes me relentlessly.

"Again. Faster this time," she orders. "Your life depends on this, Aurora. Hesitate for even a second, and you're dead."

I set my feet and raise the gun again, my arms aching, weariness and frustration simmering inside me. And this time, with ruthless precision, I empty the entire magazine into the target's chest and head in seconds. Putting down the gun, I rip off the earmuffs and glare at Hadria.

"Fast enough for you?"

Hadria arches one eyebrow, surprised by my defiant tone. For a tense moment, we stare at each other. Then, inexplicably, Hadria smiles.

"Not bad."

Her praise catches me off guard. Unsure how to respond, I simply nod my thanks. Hadria steps closer, gray eyes intent on my face. "Where was that when you were shooting at me?"

"I…" How to explain that I was shaking so hard I could barely keep the gun level?

But thankfully, she doesn't seem to expect a response, going on, "You've got potential, Aurora. We'll continue your training tomorrow."

I'm absurdly pleased by her words. Hadria studies me a moment longer, her gaze lingering on my mouth. The air suddenly seems to crackle between us. She sways incrementally closer...

And abruptly, she steps back. "Now off you go."

I stand there for a moment, confused and disappointed, before I realize I've been summarily dismissed. I have to fight the urge to run as I turn away, and manage to keep to a fast walk as I return up the stairs.

For a brief moment down there, I thought...

I thought Hadria was going to kiss me.

CHAPTER 14

Hadria

MUCH LATER THAT NIGHT, when dawn is coming close, I'm alone again in the windowless war room, head throbbing as I go over the latest requests from outside entities. Vengeance… murder…blood. That's all that ever seems to surround me.

Those moments with Aurora earlier were self-indulgent.

But I enjoyed them, all the same.

I dig my fingertips into my temples in a futile attempt to relieve the pounding pressure, because there's always more work to be done—planning tomorrow's interruption of my brother's shipments through the docks. Another mosquito intended to bite and irritate, but I want to keep up the pressure. He's gone to ground since I stole his bride, too difficult to catch in the open.

But I don't want him to think for a moment that I've forgotten about him.

Yet my thoughts drift back inevitably to the delicate face and questioning blue eyes of my captive. The mere thought of her stirs a pulsing warmth low in my belly. I close my eyes, recalling the satin warmth of her skin under my hands as I adjusted her grip on the pistol. The way her lithe, tempting body pressed back against me, my chest pressed against her shoulder blades. The scent of her soft hair—

The door pushes open. I recognize the heavy tread of boots and jangle of hardware even before Lyssa enters. She ambles over, looking irritable. "Another day in paradise, eh, Boss?"

Before I can respond, Lyssa thumps a bottle of whiskey onto the table in front of me with a dull thud. Amber liquid sloshes audibly, and she fetches two glasses from the cabinet at the side of the room.

"Drink up," she says. "We've got personal shit to discuss." She splashes three generous fingers into each glass and shoves one towards me.

I shove it back decisively, splashing some onto the table's worn surface. "I don't have time for your drunken antics. There's still work to be done."

Lyssa ignores my glower and downs her whiskey in one long swallow, exhaling gustily. "Yeah, yeah, mobsters and *bratva* and existential dilemmas. Now drink up before I pour this whole bottle down your throat myself."

I consider punishing her outrageous insubordination. But the whiskey does look tempting, and Lyssa has proven a sympathetic ear during my more reflective moods in the past. I take the proffered glass and sip, letting it spread through my chest in a molten trickle.

My guests never fail to remark on the quality of the stock I keep, from weapons to booze to assassins. And Lyssa is definitely the best of the latter, so as I wait for my best alcohol to work its magic on my mood, she knows better than to interrupt my thoughts. We drink in contemplative silence for a long moment.

Finally, reluctantly, I speak. "I don't know what I was thinking with the girl today."

Lyssa tilts her head, dark eyes glinting. "You mean your new bedwarmer?"

I bristle at once, and she smirks. "Don't talk about her like that," I warn her. "She asked me to show her how to be strong, and I said that I would."

"Mm-hmm." Lyssa's knowing look says she clearly perceives there was far more primal motivation behind my actions.

I forge on, ignoring her silent implication. "You were right about one thing. It was foolish to get so…close." Unbidden, my pulse quickens remembering Aurora pressed so intimately against me. "I want you to take over her weapons training moving forward."

Lyssa's eyebrows lift, but she seems for once to sense I require delicacy in this matter. "Probably for the best, if you're determined she has it. You've got enough on your plate." Her words lack any real mockery.

I nod tersely and finish my drink, craving the numbness of inebriation now to dull this unwelcome ache of unfulfilled desire. And Lyssa seems to read my mind, refilling our glasses, splashing more generously this time. She leans back with her refreshed drink, glancing at me sideways.

"If you want her, *have* her," she says baldly. "She wouldn't resist. She wants you, too. She drenches herself every time you look her way. I can practically smell it."

"Delightful."

She shrugs. "And true."

The whiskey has loosened my tongue enough to answer her with more candor than I'd normally allow. "I want her," I admit. "But I know if I touch her…"

"What?" Lyssa prompts at last.

"I'll destroy that light in her eyes." With a sigh, I take another sip. "There's something in me that would take great pleasure in extinguishing it, Lyssa. That's why I can't be around her."

Lyssa snorts. "You're just worried it would actually *mean* something to you."

I wish that was all it was. And yes, maybe Lyssa is onto

something. But it's more than that, too. There's this darkness in me that wants…

Not to *take* Aurora.

But to break her.

When I don't respond, Lyssa presses on. "I've watched you with her, you know. I see how gentle you are, the way you make sure her needs are met. And she's grateful for your kindnesses."

"I don't intend to take advantage of that gratitude." I shift again, discomfited by Lyssa's astute observations. It's true Aurora has wanted for nothing since being brought to the estate. I've seen that she's been treated well—given suitable clothes, books, music. Access to the grounds and gardens, as much as possible.

Small comforts that I tell myself are necessary to keep her compliant, but are actually just to make *me* feel less guilty for the things I want to do for her.

Lyssa sighs. "Oh, face facts, Hadria. You've got a soft spot for the girl, that's all. A few nights in bed with her and you'd get rid of the craving."

I'm taken aback by the savage response that rises up in me at Lyssa's casual dismissal, and I cover it up by draining my glass and thumping it down on the table. "Enough. All I want from you is to see her properly trained. She may need those skills sooner than we know, if Nero manages to gather his forces."

At this, Lyssa frowns. "Giving her a gun if he tries to break in here might not work out the way you think it will."

Rage rises hot and involuntary in my chest, and my response comes out more heated than I intend. "Of course it would! She *hates* him!"

She gives me a speculative look, reading my reaction too clearly. "No," she says softly. "*You* hate him. The girl barely knows him. You want my advice?" She goes on before I can tell her no. "Stop mooning around. Fuck her if you want, but get that strategic mind of yours back in the game. We started this war for a goddamn reason. And if you're not careful, we'll lose it."

"Then stop needling me and go do your job!" I snarl.

Lyssa's eyes widen briefly at my vehemence before she smooths her expression. "As you say, Boss." She drains her glass, eyeing me thoughtfully. When she speaks again, her words are uncharacteristically gentle. "Just be careful, okay? I'd hate to see this girl become your undoing. Not after everything we've worked for."

She stands and leaves, while I continue rolling my empty glass between my palms, watching fractured light play across the crystal.

Lyssa means well, but there are some paths a ruler must walk alone. Aurora has awakened something dangerously alluring within me—something I both fear and ache for in equal measure.

But I cannot unmake my choices now...and nor would I wish to, because they've finally born fruit. I received a message earlier today that Nero wants to parley.

And that Papa has offered to mediate between us.

CHAPTER 15

Aurora

I WAKE up to a curt knock at the door, completely unlike the way Angie or Mrs. Graves come in with my breakfast each morning—or rather, evening. Before I can sleepily respond, Lyssa barges in, dressed in her usual black leather pants and close-clinging black t-shirt.

"Wake up, little Suzy. Time to rise and shine and get your ass downstairs for training."

I sit up, pulling the blankets around me. "I thought Hadria was going to train me?"

Lyssa scoffs. "The Boss has more important things to do than play teacher. Now get dressed, unless you want me to drag your scrawny ass out of bed myself."

Disappointment wells up inside me, but I swallow it down and get up. I dress quickly and follow Lyssa down the long hallway. She doesn't speak, doesn't even glance back at me. But then, Lyssa has never made any effort to hide her disdain for my presence here.

In her eyes, I suppose I'm an interloper. An outsider. I don't belong here.

Well…we're in agreement there.

We descend to the underground shooting range. The muffled blasts of gunfire greet us. I'm not the only one here today. Lyssa hands me the earmuffs again and leads me into the sleek, concrete-walled space. Faceless paper targets stand at the far end, already riddled with holes from previous trainees. There are at least four of them still here, all men, all glancing over their shoulders at me as I passed, checking me out with expressions ranging from bewilderment to scorn.

Without preamble, Lyssa places a handgun in my palm—not the small, easily managed one Hadria allowed me to use yesterday, but something heavier, more substantial.

"Let's see if you can actually hit anything with a big girl gun, Suzy."

I want to snap at her not to call me that, but I focus on the task. The gun sits heavily in my hand, the grip unfamiliar. But as I raise my arms and stare down the barrel at the distant target, Hadria's lessons come back to me. Inhale, exhale, squeeze the trigger on the exhale. *Don't yank.* The sharp crack of the gunshot rings out, and a neat hole appears in the shoulder of the paper target, despite the harder recoil.

"Beginner's luck," Lyssa mutters. But I block her out, steadying my breath, recalling Hadria's guidance. I empty the gun, each shot landing closer to the bullseye in the chest, until the final one punches straight through its heart.

I lower the gun, unable to keep a small, satisfied smile from my lips. Lyssa says nothing, but her eyebrows lift ever so slightly. It's probably the closest I'll get to praise from her.

The morning passes in a blur of gun smoke and ringing shots. Lyssa pushes me hard, having me try different firearms, firing on the move, shooting while she attempts to distract me. I miss more than I hit, but find myself gaining confidence. There's something soothing about the repetitive motion, the focus it requires.

By eleven, Lyssa declares the shooting portion done. I feel a flicker of pride at having completed the grueling session without complaint. But it is quickly extinguished when Lyssa says our next stop is the gym.

I've never been what you'd call sporty, and the spacious gymnasium is a hive of activity. Men and a few women spar around the gym, their grunts and the dull smack of fists on flesh echoing off the concrete walls. Weights clank and treadmills whirr. These are *all* new recruits, I realize. Hadria must be expanding her forces.

Their eyes follow me as I enter, raking over me with undisguised curiosity and contempt. They nudge each other, chuckling. I recognize the dismissal in their gazes from the trainees at the gun range this morning. I'm merely a girl, out of my depth. Anger bubbles up, especially when I see how deferential they are to Lyssa.

Lyssa gathers a group of recruits and leads us through some basic self-defense moves: how to block a strike, use an opponent's momentum against them, create space to allow escape. They're rudimentary but useful. She moves into a few attack basics next, and we practice them along with her: straight punch, knee-kick, side-kick.

Then Lyssa announces I'll be sparring with one of the recruits. "Try not to embarrass yourself too much, Suzy," she says in an undertone.

At least she didn't say it loud enough for everyone to hear.

A broad-shouldered young man steps forward, muscle straining under his sleeveless shirt. "This should be quick," he says, eliciting laughter from the others. I clench my jaw, meeting his smug gaze.

We take positions on the mat as the others form a makeshift ring around us. Lyssa steps back, arms crossed, face unreadable.

"Go easy on her, Mario," one of the recruits calls out. More laughter. Mario's mouth curls into a cocky grin.

"I'll try not to bruise that pretty face of yours, sweetheart," he says.

Rage sparks through me at the casual disrespect. But I rein it in, letting it smolder.

Mario moves with lumbering slowness, aiming a punch at my right cheek that I deftly dodge, dancing back out of reach. He charges again and I use his momentum to send him stumbling past me. But he recovers quickly, fueled by the whoops and jeers of the crowd.

"Not bad, sweetheart," he pants, circling me. "But you won't get lucky again."

He feints left then strikes right, and pain explodes along my jaw. I crash to the mat, head ringing. The men roar their approval. Through the haze I see Mario looming above me, grinning.

"Stay down, sweetheart. No need to embarrass yourself further."

His words pour gasoline on my simmering anger. It erupts into an inferno, hot and hungry. I surge to my feet, the pain forgotten, as Lyssa's instructions from earlier come flooding back to me. Mario's eyes widen in surprise an instant before my fist connects with his solar plexus. He doubles over with a choked grunt and I bring my knee up, catching him in the nose. He reels backwards, and a final side-kick at his knee sees him crash to the mat.

Silence rings out. I stand over Mario, chest heaving, and spit his own words back at him. "Stay down, sweetheart. No need to embarrass yourself further."

The recruits stare at me, mouths agape. And then they all start laughing hysterically.

Even Mario, when I stretch out a hand to help him to his feet, is giving a rueful grin. "Yeah, yeah," he grumbles at the other recruits. "Laugh it up. Wait till Suzy here gets ahold of you."

Out of the corner of my eye, I see Lyssa regarding me with narrowed eyes and the barest hint of a smile.

"Well, well. Seems like you've got a little fire in you after all, Suzy Sunshine. Though I suppose the sun is just one big ball of angry fire, isn't it?" she adds with a smirk.

Adrenaline still thrums through me, but as I look at Mario holding his head back and trying to stop his nosebleed, the full impact of what I've done hits me.

I unleashed violence on another person. And it was shockingly easy.

Even…even *fun*.

Lyssa disperses the onlooking recruits and leads me from the gym. I'm trembling now, overwhelmed. She guides me to a small room just off the training area and pushes me down onto a bench.

"Breathe, Suzy. You won the fight—and a little respect along with it." Her tone is not unkind. She hands me a towel to wipe the sweat from my brow.

I take a few deep breaths, regaining some composure. The whirlwind of emotions still rages within me—anger, shock, and beneath it all, a disquieting sense of satisfaction.

I defended myself. Proved I'm not as weak as they assumed.

Lyssa sits beside me, leaning forward with her elbows on her knees. "Not gonna lie, I didn't expect you to have that in you. Wasn't sure you had the spine for this world."

I meet her brown eyes. "I won't be anyone's victim again."

She nods slowly. "Good. Because this place will chew you up and spit you out otherwise." She stands abruptly. "I'll let you go clean up, get some food. Training's done for today."

As she turns to leave, I find myself saying, "Will you tell Hadria what I did? Do you think—do you think she'll be pleased?"

Lyssa stills, then looks back at me with an inscrutable expression. "Hadria appreciates strength. But don't go looking for her approval, Suzy. That's a losing game. You just focus on surviving."

With that, she leaves me with my thoughts swirling. I move to the small adjoining bathroom and wash the blood—Mario's and my own—from my hands and face.

The woman staring back at me from the mirror looks different, somehow. Harder.

This place will chew you up and spit you out, Lyssa warned me. But I won't be so easily consumed. I survived my father's cruelty, and I will survive this.

If I'm to have any power over my fate, I must continue training, hone my body and mind. I'll observe and learn the ways of this world that has claimed me.

And when the time is right, I will free myself.

CHAPTER 16

Hadria

I STARE at my reflection in the full-length mirror, straightening my black silk tie. The sleek designer suit I chose fits my tall, lean frame perfectly, the gunmetal fabric crisp and well-tailored. I cut an imposing figure. Powerful. Authoritative.

Every inch the ruthless Boss I've fought to become.

Tonight I need that aura of cold command more than ever. This meeting with my brother and father will be a pivotal power play, a challenge to their patriarchal bullshit.

And I fully intend to come out on top.

A knock at the door draws my gaze away from the mirror. "Come in," I call, my voice steady despite the tension coiling through my muscles.

Lyssa enters, scanning me up and down. "Looking sharp, Boss. You ready to bust some balls tonight?"

"Bold of you to assume they have any balls worth busting."

She barks out a laugh. "True. Maybe you should aim a little higher. Like a knife to the gut." Her smile sharpens. "Metaphorically speaking, of course."

Trust Lyssa to get right to the heart of things…and with no delicacy whatsoever. It's why she's one of the few I trust. Her violent tendencies make her ruthlessly efficient, but she's always had my back, ever since she dragged me out from under a group of drunken men my very first night on the streets, and told me I needed to toughen up.

And then she showed me what she meant, by gutting the three men and looting their bodies for wallets and watches.

Lyssa was absolutely right. My privileged upbringing was a disadvantage to me. I was soft and clueless. But thanks to people like Lyssa and Mrs. Graves, who took the two of us in off the street after we avenged the murder of her only daughter, I *did* toughen up.

I broke myself apart and reforged those pieces into a new being: Hades. And as I grew in power and legend, I was able to pay back Lyssa and Mrs. Graves ten times over, so that now they live in wealth and luxury, though they've both retained their diamond-hard cores.

And tonight is the final chapter of what I like to think of as my origin story. I'll get to face my father and show him how wrong he was to choose Nero over me, just because of the soft thing that hangs between his legs.

Best case scenario? Papa will beg my forgiveness, plead with me to come back to the Imperioli Family, and lead it into the same greatness into which I led the Styx Syndicate.

Worst case scenario…

Well, I suppose I should think positive.

I adjust my cufflinks, platinum and diamond. "I have no intention of playing nice tonight," I assure Lyssa.

She nods. "About damn time."

"Have the car brought around. And double security presence here tonight at Elysium, just in case Nero thinks it would be clever to attack while we're away. I don't want any surprises."

Lyssa salutes mockingly. "You got it, Boss." She pauses at the door, glancing back. "Watch yourself tonight. Don't let those bastards get under your skin. Keep that cool head of yours, Hades."

When I descend to the foyer some minutes later, I am ready. Chin high, shoulders square, power in every step.

Mrs. Graves waits at the open front door, her face showing pride, but a little concern underneath. "Good luck, Hadria."

I put a hand on her arm. "Thank you." Her concern reminds me I have people counting on me. Relying on me to secure my legacy once and for all. Because in turn, that means I'll be able to secure *their* safety, too.

Aurora is one of those people.

Outside, the sleek black town car idles in the drive, flanked fore and aft by additional vehicles bearing my personal security team. Lyssa holds the rear door open, waving me in with a smile and a flourish.

She leans down to give me a wink, and then goes over the details again, even though we've discussed them a thousand times. "The meeting's set for Valentino's as usual." Valentino's is an upscale Italian restaurant downtown that caters exclusively to the elite of Chicago's underworld. I've held countless meetings there. "I'll ride with the security convoy. We'll sweep the place beforehand, cover all entrances and exits. Any problems won't be problems by the time you get in there."

I nod, glimpsing her shoulder holster and the way her suit jacket drapes just so to conceal the weapon. Lyssa enjoys killing, and she's exceptionally good at it. "Let's hope your skills aren't required."

She shrugs. "You know me, always itching for a little action." With a sly grin, she shuts the door.

As the car glides through the wrought-iron gates toward downtown Chicago, I focus on controlling my breathing. In through the nose, out through the mouth. Pulse steady. Nerves ice. The mannerisms of power must come naturally, or the perception of authority crumbles.

I cannot allow even a shred of weakness, not with so much at stake.

And I absolutely cannot afford to think of Aurora. I've made every effort to avoid her for the last few days in preparation for this meeting, even though Lyssa tells me she's making good progress in her training.

No. The last thing I need right now is that soft little warmth in my belly that I get when I think about Aurora.

The city skyline grows closer as we close in on downtown, and we eventually descend into the underground valet area of Valentino's.

Lyssa accompanies me in the elevator, and steps out first at the restaurant, scanning for threats before nodding me through. My security team fans out, establishing a perimeter around the place. I saunter into the dim, elegant interior of the restaurant.

The maître d' straightens, recognition glinting in his eyes. "Ms. Imperioli, so good to see you." For a long time I never used my surname. But tonight it feels right. It feels right to hear my real name, a name that I am still proud of, said in that deferential tone. "Please, come this way."

At Valentino's, an environment of privacy and discretion is paramount. I follow the maître d' through the near-empty dining room, heading for one of the private back rooms. It's still early, the evening crowd yet to arrive, but I glimpse two broad-shouldered figures seated at a table in a secluded alcove room. My brother, Nero, and our father, Zepp—Giuseppe really, but everyone calls him Zepp.

I quickly master the spike of anger their silhouettes evoke. Now is not the time for passion. A cool head and cutting intellect are my most potent weapons.

The maître d' pauses at the alcove entrance. "Your guests have been awaiting your arrival. Please let me know if you require anything further."

As he retreats, I school my expression to cold neutrality.

With a final steeling breath, I step around the corner into the alcove.

Showtime.

Nero and my father look up at my entrance, their faces like thunderclouds. I read their anger, their disapproval, their grudging respect in the tense lines around their mouths, the flat stares.

Good. Let them churn.

"Hadria," Nero greets me first, biting off the word. "So good of you to finally join us."

I arch an eyebrow. "Business never starts without me, little brother." Pulling out the chair opposite them both, I seat myself, back straight, never breaking eye contact. The power play of making them wait was petty, sure—but effective. Especially on Nero, who is an impatient hothead. Tonight, I want my father to truly understand what a weakness Nero's hot temper really is.

As for Papa, he remains silent, bushy eyebrows drawn down as he observes me. An alpha wolf, sizing me up.

After an interminable silence, Nero speaks again. "I believe you know why we asked to meet."

"As a matter of fact, I don't," I reply tonelessly. "Unless Papa finally plans to admit he made a mistake all those years ago when he named you his heir?"

Nero's face mottles, restraint splintering already. "You took what is mine." He spits the words.

I can't resist prodding the wound. "Took what, dear brother? Your masculinity?" I signal the watching waiter for a drink. "I thought that shriveled prune was lost long ago."

Before Nero can combust, Papa slams a fist on the table, making the silverware jump, and Nero, too. But not me. "Enough." His voice is grave thunder. "This has to stop, Hadria."

I smile without humor, leaning back casually in my seat as I accept the red wine from the waiter. I take a slow sip, and when I meet my father's glower again, my face is a mask of innocence.

"You'll have to forgive me. I was unaware there was anything serious to discuss, except for my rightful claim to the Imperioli Family."

Zepp shakes his head. "That's what it's about for you, eh? The same, endless tantrum you had as a teenager."

"If you still think Nero will be an effective successor to you, Papa, then you must have developed dementia since we last met."

He stabs a finger at me. "You show me respect, girl," he growls. "My decision was final. I cannot leave the Family to a woman; the idea is absurd. And in any case, you deserted us long ago."

"No," I say. "*You* turned your back on *me*. And I'm here tonight for your apology."

Papa waves an impatient hand, brushing my words aside with an irritated look. "The past is past. Now, there are matters we must resolve."

This is the first time my father has seen me since I disappeared, nearly sixteen years ago. Not a single question about how I am. Not a single flicker of regret in his eyes.

It seems as though he would simply have preferred me gone forever.

Nero jumps in again. "Yeah, we have shit to sort out—like you abducting my fiancée on my wedding day. Inciting unrest with our allies. Endangering *everything* our Family has built." He ticks off each accusation on his fingers, nearly shaking with outrage.

I take another sip of wine before replying. "Endangering the Imperioli Family? I built the Syndicate with a view to strengthening the Family. What I offer is an alliance. All my wealth, all my soldiers, all my mercenaries for hire. As long as I'm named heir to the Imperiolis. While you…" I give him a disdainful glance. "What do you have to offer the Family, apart from drunken lechery?"

Nero halfway lurches out of his chair, murder in his eyes. Zepp captures his arm in an iron grip, yanking him back down. "Sit. Down," he grates. Nero seethes but complies.

Zepp turns his attention back to me. The guise of mediator has slipped. He speaks quietly, intently. "Hadria, this childishness must end. And so must this running around Chicago pretending to be some—some hardened mercenary. I would welcome you back to the Family, you know that I would. But not as a leader." He pauses, exhaling through flared nostrils. "And not while this insult to Nero stands. You must return the girl to him."

"If you have a problem with it, speak to Jimmy Verderosa. He's the one who offered his daughter to me years before he tried to sell her to Nero." I shrug. "I simply collected what was owed to me."

Nero scoffs. "You expect us to believe that? Jimmy told us he ain't got any clue what you're talking about." His lip curls in disgust. "And what the hell do you want with her, anyway?"

I allow a cryptic little smile to play about my lips. "Oh, we've become quite...intimate. She's proven *most* satisfying." I put a lurid emphasis into my words, and have the pleasure of watching Nero's expression curdle with rage.

An eternal weakness, that rage of his.

And yet...I feel a strange discomfort speaking of Aurora like this. In front of anyone else, I wouldn't. And if I heard anyone saying something similar, they would soon lose their ability to speak at all.

Before Nero can retort, Zepp slams the table again. "Goddamn it, girl, this isn't a game!" His composure finally cracks, revealing exhaustion and frustration. "Give up this foolish crusade. Make peace with your brother. For the good of the Family."

For an instant, I feel an unexpected twinge of remorse,

seeing the toll our contest of wills has taken. He *is* still my father, after all. The man whose approval I so badly crave.

But I crush the sensation ruthlessly. Sentiment will gain me nothing here. What I want is *power*. Power and formal recognition.

Leaning forward, I meet Papa's eyes, my voice glacial and precise. "The good of this Family? You dare speak to me of family, when you always valued this fool over me?" I flick my gaze disdainfully at Nero. "I might have left, Papa, but it was you who cast me aside. And now I have a new Family, people who are loyal to the death...unlike *you*."

At that, Papa chuckles. "You don't have a new Family, girl. Mercenaries are only loyal to one thing: money. You have a group of people who'll put up with you ordering them around until someone pays them more than you do—and then you'll end up with a blade in your back."

I push back from the table and stand, straightening my jacket with savage tugs, and remind myself that I did mentally prepare for this outcome, even if I hoped for something better. "I'm not a girl, Don Imperioli. I am a grown woman and I intend to take the Family from you, if you won't give it willingly." I give my coldest smile. "Or I'll kill every last member of it before I see a weak, impotent fool like Nero inherit what is rightfully mine."

Nero stares up at me, slack-jawed. But my father's expression hardens, grudging respect mingling with the outrage in his eyes.

"So that's how it is, then?" he asks softly. His hands clench to fists atop the pristine white tablecloth, knuckles bone-white. "You'd threaten your own father's legacy, everything I built, to satisfy your petty jealousy?"

"If I were you, I'd think carefully about my offer, Papa. I've been preparing for war for a long time." I turn to Nero with a sneer. "See you on the battlefield, little brother."

He stands, throwing off our father's restraining hand. "Oh,

I'll be there, bitch. Make sure the girl is, too, because the first time I fuck her, I want to do it on top of *your goddamn corpse!*"

Turning on my heel, I stride from the alcove room, not deigning to glance back.

Righteous fury carries me back out into the hushed restaurant, and everyone there must have heard my brother's crude shout. The waitstaff averts their eyes, not daring to meet my gaze.

I keep my shoulders rigid until I reach the elevator with Lyssa, who mutters, "Well, that went well." I don't respond, barely let out a breath until I'm back in the car. Only once settled back against the leather seat, the tinted windows concealing me from prying eyes, do I allow myself to release the tension in a long, shuddering exhale.

Lyssa slides in opposite me, reading the signs of a confrontation. "So…we go to war?"

I give an almost imperceptible nod, staring fixedly out the window as the car pulls away from the curb. She takes the hint, thank God, settling back without another word.

I watch the city lights stream by in silence, trying to quiet my mind by replaying each exchanged barb and threat. Despite Nero's outrage and father's blustering disapproval, they know now I am utterly serious about taking control of the Family. Of the city. By any means necessary.

My path is set. All that remains is to eliminate any obstacles. Starting with my dear baby brother.

When I have him at my mercy, I will slowly and brutally castrate him and then watch him bleed out, because his threat toward Aurora has driven all thoughts of restraint from my mind.

No one threatens what is mine.

CHAPTER 17
Aurora

IT'S A NEAR-FULL MOON TONIGHT, rising above the treetops as its silver glow bathes the flower beds in the night garden. The intoxicating fragrances of night-blooming jasmine and flowering tobacco mingle on the gentle breeze, enveloping me in their heady perfumes.

When training is done for the night, or if Lyssa and the other recruits have gone out on scouting missions—I've never even tried to suggest I might go along on one of them—then I come out here and let myself reconnect to that other version of me, the one who still loves plants and flowers, who relishes the feeling of soft soil between her toes. This is a place that makes me feel like a magical fairy princess...instead of a hostage. When I tend the beds of angel's trumpets and evening primroses, their velvety petals soft beneath my fingertips, I can almost forget that I'm a captive here.

Almost.

Tonight, most of the Syndicate is out. Lyssa and Hadria and a whole fleet of cars left the grounds earlier. I snuck down to the foyer as they were leaving and watched them go. I wonder where—

A crunch of gravel underfoot startles me from my reverie. I whirl around to see Hadria standing at the edge of the path, half-cloaked in shadows. My heart leaps into my throat.

She looks every inch the crime lord she is in that close-cut suit. From her jet-black hair to her intense, angular features, her whole appearance screams *Danger! Danger!*

But there's an uncertainty in her stance as she moves forward into a pool of moonlight, at odds with her usual commanding presence.

"This place—it's *beautiful*." Even her voice is uncharacteristically hesitant. "I didn't realize this was what you were doing out here each night." She looks around, eyebrows raised, and then takes a step back. "But I've disturbed you. I'm sorry."

I push my hair out of my eyes, bouncing up to my feet. "Oh, please stay! I love being out here and it's…well, it's nice to have someone to share it with."

Part of me thrills at this private audience with her, the woman who has dominated my thoughts since I arrived here.

The other part is wondering if I can turn this moment to my advantage.

I'm not good at being manipulative. It doesn't come naturally to me. But it's another skill I'm going to have to learn if I want to survive here.

If I want to grasp my freedom.

Hadria steps forward beside me, still glancing around at the improvements I've made in the night garden. "I didn't even know this could be so beautiful," she murmurs. For a moment she seems entranced by the garden's nocturnal blooms, her sharp features softening as she inhales their heady scent. She looks younger, unguarded.

Almost vulnerable.

My soft heart turns traitor, aching at this glimpse beneath her hardened exterior. What must it have cost her, to lock so much of herself away under that armor?

"You've done wonders with this place," she says. "It was overgrown and dead when you arrived. Now it's…" She trails off, at a loss for words.

"Now it has a chance to thrive," I finish with a small smile.

Hadria looks at me keenly. Despite her aloofness these past weeks, I still sense her fascination with me—one that mirrors my own tangled feelings towards her. Heat rises in my cheeks and I turn aside to hide it.

"Do you need anything else to tend to it?" she asks. "More supplies?"

I'm touched by her thoughtfulness, even though I try to remind myself that she's my captor. "A few more bags of potting soil would be useful," I reply after a moment. "And better pruning shears. The ones I have are dull." I hold up the shears, suddenly self-conscious asking anything of her. But she simply nods again.

"I'll have the staff fetch whatever you need. Give Mrs. Graves a list, and she'll get it done for you."

"Thank you."

She hesitates a moment and then says, "If you really would like me to stay, I wonder if there's something I can do to…help? I've no idea about plants, but I could hand you whatever tools you need."

Hadria Imperioli has no interest in gardening, that much I know. But she has something she wants to say, clearly, and I'm curious. "Sure," I say, and point at the trowel. "Pass me that?"

We work in companionable silence, Hadria handing me tools while I trim and shape the night-blooming bushes. It's strange at first, Hadria playing nurse to my surgeon. This garden is the one place where I feel in control. Where I can shape the environment to my will, coaxing beauty from the earth. It's a small triumph, but one that empowers me in the midst of all these overpowering forces.

And I want it to be beautiful for *her*, though I'm not entirely sure why. Maybe I just want to prove to her that even in the ugliest of times, there can be small pockets of beauty.

"I've been out tonight," she says at last. I say nothing, unwilling to interrupt. Whatever she has to say, it's about to come out. "I met with my father and my brother. Nero."

I dead-head a rose with a decisive snip of my shears. "I see."

"My father still refuses to depose my brother in favor of me," she goes on, and then waits for my reaction.

I stand up straight from the bush I've been leaning over and look at her. "But you expected that," I say slowly, reading her face.

She gives a small smile. "Perhaps even hoped for it. It gives me an excuse to escalate, you see. But…" Her face goes grave. "Aurora, you need to promise me something. You need to work hard on your self-defense lessons with Lyssa. Because if the unthinkable happens—if I fail, which I won't, but…if I do…" She pauses, as though even admitting the idea of failure is painful to her. "If Nero comes to claim you again, you need to kill him. Because if you don't, very soon after he takes you back, you will wish *you* were dead. He's an animal. There's no trace of humanity left in him. Your innocence won't give him pause like —" She breaks off.

"Like it does you?" I say after a moment.

Hadria is very close to me now, so that I have to look up into her face. She reaches out to brush an errant curl from my cheek. "Yes," she says simply.

"May I ask you something?" I venture finally.

Hadria tenses, her expression shuttering closed. But she nods for me to continue.

"Why do you and Nero hate each other so much?"

For a moment I fear she'll retreat back into silence. But to my surprise, she sinks down on a stone bench, gesturing for me to join her.

"You should know the truth," she says heavily. "Your life has been swallowed up by my feud with my brother. You deserve to understand why."

I sit beside her, breathless with anticipation. Never before has she spoken so openly. As I study her profile, I am struck again by her cruel beauty.

Dangerous, yet difficult to resist.

"From the time we were children, Nero was groomed to lead the Family. As the eldest, it should have been *my* birthright. But..." She trails off, jaw tight.

"But you were born a woman," I finish softly.

Her eyes flash. "No matter what I did, my father saw me as weak, unfit to rule. No matter how I strove to prove myself, it was never enough." She laughs bitterly. "Even now, with an empire of my own, he still believes Nero is the rightful heir— not because he's in any way suited to it, but because he has a worm between his legs."

I do understand her rage, which is unmistakable, though icy. Her relentless pursuit of power, her refusal to bend to any man's will...I get it. In fact, she represents the very same freedom I crave. The freedom to live by my own strength.

To never again be at the mercy of another person's whims.

"I'm sorry," I murmur. Before I can second guess myself, I place my hand over hers where it rests tensely on her knee. She inhales sharply but doesn't pull away. Surprise flickers across her face, followed by another unreadable emotion.

She studies my face, as if trying to make sense of me. We stare at each other as the air seems to hum between us, electric and alive.

And then Hadria clears her throat and glances aside, leaning away a little on the stone bench. The spell is broken.

"When I realized my father wouldn't budge on Nero, I left. I made a new life for myself, living on the streets—that's where I met Lyssa. She taught me how to take care of myself. To fight. To *win*. That's why," she adds, fixing me with her gaze again, "I wanted her to teach you, too. Because she's better than me at that sort of thing. Not saying I'm unskilled in any way," she says with a laugh as she sees my eyebrows go up, "but Lyssa is a born warrior. Me, I'm more of a strategist."

"Like a General," I say. "In the army."

Her smile suggests that she likes that idea. "And so with my gift for strategy and Lyssa's natural talents, the two of us started to become known as…well, as fixers, I suppose. We were the people you came to when you had a problem. In those days, it was small things. Local store owners might ask us to take care of regular shoplifters. Or we'd act as protection at underground lesbian events. But one day, Mrs. Graves came to us. Her daughter had been killed, and she knew exactly who had done it —but the man was in a gang. He had a score of witnesses putting him somewhere else at the time, and so the charges didn't stick. She asked us to give her vengeance."

"And you did," I say, entranced by the story.

Hadria inclines her head. "We did. And Mrs. Graves took us in after that. Housed us. Fed us. Mothered us, I suppose."

"What happened to your own mother?" I ask without thinking.

Hadria stares at the flowers for a long moment before saying, "She died when I was young. She was collateral damage in a hit against my father."

"I—I'm so sorry—"

"Lyssa tells me you are progressing in your training."

I let her change the subject. "Yes. I'm quick; quicker than the boys. They lumber around, but I'm much faster than them. And Lyssa says I have a natural talent for shooting."

I can't help boasting. The training has empowered me, awakening strengths I never knew I had. I'm moving further and further away from the timid little girl who submitted silently to life's tides.

And I want Hadria to approve of me, despite Lyssa's warning.

Hadria's lips quirk upward. "That's high praise coming from the Wolf. Perhaps you might sit in on a Syndicate meeting soon." She pauses, adds casually, "If you like."

"I would like that very much," I assure her.

Her fingers brush tentatively over mine in a feather-light caress. "Good. And now I should leave you to your gardening." She stands, gives me a little nod. "Good night, Aurora."

"Good night, Hadria."

I watch her silhouette fade into the shadows and find myself trembling. With fear? Anticipation? Or something else entirely?

I don't know.

But I feel myself changing, reshaping, coming alive, just like the night garden under my hands.

CHAPTER 18

Aurora

I SMOOTH the sleek black fabric of my skirt, my nerves making my hands tremble. Today—tonight—I'll be attending my first Syndicate meeting, about a week after Hadria first suggested it. The thought thrills me, even as anxiety flutters in my chest. I want to prove myself, to show Hadria I can be useful, that I belong in her world.

I want her to *trust* me.

In the mirror, I critically examine my appearance. My white blouse is pressed crisp, waist nipped in by a high-waisted pencil skirt. A far cry from the diaphanous wedding dress I wore on the day most of the Syndicate members last saw me. I sweep my hair up into a ponytail, like the kind Lyssa wears when she goes out to work, and I stare hard at my face. I've used a bright orange-red lipstick that I hope looks sophisticated, and only added a touch of mascara to my eyes. Anything more and I'd feel like a clown.

But anything less, and I'd look too young and innocent.

A knock interrupts my primping: Lyssa has arrived to escort me. The tall blonde sweeps into my room, eyes taking in every detail.

"Well, well, look who cleans up okay," she remarks. "Won't hurt to have some eye candy at the table."

I bristle slightly at the implication I'm only there for decoration, but Lyssa's biting humor is the closest she gets to a compliment. I'll take what I can get.

"And it goes with saying that you'll keep those painted lips sealed and your ears open," she adds pointedly. I nod, and she gives me a critical look. "You know, Suzy, I think Hadria's making a mistake with you. You might *look* like some delicate flower with nothing between the ears, but I think you know exactly what you're doing. If it was up to me, you'd be kept chained up in a dungeon somewhere, instead of allowed to roam free-range."

I lift my chin. "Good thing it's not up to you, then, isn't it? It's up to Hadria."

Lyssa stares at me for a long moment before giving that wild, strange laugh. "One day you'll sass the wrong person at the wrong time, Suzy. Pray it's not me. Come on."

I fall into step behind her. We travel the now-familiar hallways and stop before the imposing doors of the war room. For the first time, my eyes fall on the engraved insignia with new understanding: a three-headed dog wreathed in thorns.

Cerberus. Of course. The guardian of the gates of hell is the insignia for the Styx Syndicate. I have to suppress a giggle at the over-the-topness of it all.

But my giggle dies fast when Lyssa pushes those doors open, ushering me into the chamber again. Hadria has not yet arrived, but her lieutenants are gathered, absorbed in tense discussions. I easily identify the most senior members among them, the ones I've picked out carefully during my nightly observation of comings and goings. I don't know any last names, but I know by now their first and code names. Tony the Taxman—it took a while for me to make sure they weren't calling him the Axman, and I still have no idea why he's called what he is—is talking in an undertone to a few men and women I assume must be part of his regular crew, from the way they all lean in to listen together, comfortably close. "Ricky Half-hands" is already seated, tapping one of the few fingers he still has left on the table, moodily staring at those hands of his. And the ice-blonde with the accent (Angie the housemaid let slip once that it's actually Romanian) I now know is called Ilona the Impaler—seriously—is pouring herself a drink from the side bar. Along with Lyssa, whom I've heard several people call "the Wolf," these are Hadria's four most trusted lieutenants, her inner circle.

I desperately want to know how they came by their names. But I haven't got the nerve up yet to ask someone who would definitely know, like Lyssa.

But the room is full of many more people than just those senior mercenaries. There are at least fifteen soldiers who I know are allotted seats at the long oak table, and another twenty or so recruits are clustered in groups around the room. Lyssa points me to stand next to Mario in the group behind her seat, the guy I bested in training. He gives me a grin and a fist-bump. To my mixed distress and delight, a lot of the recruits have started calling him "Sweetheart" in reference to my taunting him with his own words that day. Thankfully, he seems to find it as funny as they do. The other trainees greet me with nods and handshakes. We're the bottom of the food chain here, especially me, but at least I've won a *little* respect from them.

A sudden hush falls over the room, and I turn to see Hadria entering from the side door, the one that leads into her office. She's clad in one of those sleek black suits that hugs her supple form, no shirt on underneath so that the jacket skims over her breasts and I have to restrain myself from staring. Her raven hair is like spun silk, falling to the tops of her shoulders in shiny waves, no matter how roughly she likes to shag it up. And her face…that compelling face could inspire poetry.

Or sins.

My pulse quickens as her pale eyes sweep the room and settle on me for a moment, before she ascends to her throne.

"Let's begin." Her clipped tone brokers no nonsense. "What's the latest intel on my brother?"

The meeting progresses swiftly. No one dares to interrupt or defy her. When tensions escalate between Tony and Ricky over security concerns, Hadria's arctic stare silences them instantly. "Figure it out," she commands.

And somehow, I know they will.

I'm rapt, studying Hadria's mastery of the room. She truly is a modern monarch.

After an hour, Ilona mentions a man called Johnny the Gentleman visiting from New York. The name elicits a few murmurs of apprehension. I lean towards Mario and whisper "Who's he?" but Lyssa turns in her chair to silence me with a sharp look. I stand up straighter, simmering with frustration at being kept in the dark.

"Keep an eye on him," is all Hadria says, and Ilona nods.

The mood turns grim as talk turns back to Nero. Tony advocates sending a violent warning, but Ricky cautions diplomacy first. Hadria listens silently, then states, "Power is the only language my brother understands. But there are many dialects to choose between."

Hadria's eyes flick to Lyssa, a subtle cue I nearly miss. Lyssa turns to me and murmurs, "You've heard enough. Time to go."

But this meeting is too important. I need to know Hadria's plans. "I want to stay," I insist under my breath.

Lyssa's glare cuts me short. "Hadria decides who stays or goes," she hisses. "Don't question it."

Her words hit their mark, silencing my protests. Hadria expects unquestioning loyalty and obedience from those who serve her. What use at all would she have for a defiant captive who doesn't know her proper place?

So I leave the group of trainees and head for the door, trying to keep my head up, but uncomfortably aware of the heat climbing up my neck and into my cheeks.

Lyssa follows me, and when I'm unable to resist a glance back at Hadria holding court over her empire, she is the one to shut the door in my face.

I stand there for a moment, frustrated, but then the door seems to crack open an inch again, and I hear Lyssa's footsteps going back to the table.

It's a clear invitation to eavesdrop, and I take it up at once, pressing up against the other door and listen for all I'm worth.

"Most of you will know who the woman who just left us is," Hadria says, her voice crisp and clear. "For those who don't: that was Aurora Verderosa, the bride I stole from my brother."

"She's a pretty little thing, that one," a man's voice cuts in with a low chuckle. "And a spitfire, I hear." There's a round of coarse laughter.

My hands ball into fists.

"Enough." Hadria's voice slices through the crude chuckles to silence them. "Aurora is not to be touched. She belongs to me. So unless you want to end up like Vinny D'Amelio, you will treat her with respect."

Vinny D'Amelio. Vinny... The name rings a bell, and I search my memory until I place it—the man who leered at me in the safe house apartment, right after Hadria first kidnapped me.

I feel a chill run through me. Vinny is...*dead?* Killed for disrespecting me? I'm not sure how I feel about that. Death seems an awfully harsh punishment just for being a creep. Though I suppose Hadria deals in harsh punishments.

It's how she got her reputation, after all.

A tense silence follows her pronouncement. I picture Hadria glaring around the table with those wintry eyes.

"I trust I've made myself clear?" she asks softly. It's not really a question.

A chorus of hasty "Yes, Boss" and "Of course, Hades" answers her. No one dares argue. And hearing her defend me so decisively also makes something warm unfurl in my chest, almost despite myself.

That warmth dies a moment later, though, as Hadria goes on.

"Aurora is proof of my dominance over Nero," she states. "She is the prize I snatched from right under his nose."

A murmur of appreciation sweeps the room at this reminder of Hadria's daring and skill.

"And now," Hadria goes on, "that prize of his is *mine*. I have taken his treasure and made it my own."

I don't like hearing her talk about me like that, reducing me to an object valued only for what I represent, not for who I am. But I stay quiet, listening intently.

"Aurora's presence here in Elysium, or at my side, sends Nero a message," says Hadria. "One I intend to reinforce at key moments. She will be seen at certain operations and events, a constant reminder to my brother that his prized bride now belongs to me. And Nero will feel the sting of it every time he sees her. She's the embodiment of my victory over him. It will drive him into a frenzy. And then…then he will make a mistake."

Of course. How did I manage to make myself forget?

To Hadria, I'm a pretty bauble to show off as a taunt to Nero. Nothing but a pawn in her chess game. Not a person with her own dreams and desires, or heart and mind.

She's no better than her brother.

I'm tempted to fling open the doors and confront her, refuse to be paraded around like an animal in a circus. But that would only undermine the precarious standing I've achieved so far. So I just stand there, fists clenched, jaw tight, as I listen to Hadria discuss me like an inanimate object.

But she's not the only one I'm mad at. Lyssa must have known exactly what Hadria was going to say tonight. And she wanted me to hear it, too.

For now, at least publicly, I know I must play the role assigned to me, bide my time. But that doesn't mean I have to accept it. Hadria intends to use me as a weapon against Nero, but weapons can be double-edged.

"My brother has reached out for another meeting," Hadria goes on. "This time, I plan to take Aurora with me. So be aware —the rabid dog might start to snap his jaws very soon, now."

There's a murmur, and then I hear the scraping of chairs again, the meeting wrapping up. Quickly I back away from the doors and run back to my room, where I pace up and down, still fuming. Eventually, it's too much for me, and I head down to the empty training room—not the shooting range; Hadria's not trusting enough to allow me free access to guns...yet—and after warming up, I go through the martial arts forms Lyssa has been drilling us with lately.

I need to focus on something physical, something that requires my complete attention. And as I go through the forms, I can feel the tension slowly seeping out of my muscles, my anger dying down as I lose myself in the motions.

Hadria wants me at this meeting with her brother as bait, nothing more, but it does give me an opportunity to understand their relationship better. And information is always valuable.

After a while, Lyssa enters the room. I obstinately keep moving through my forms, and she watches me silently. When I finish my routine, I turn to face her. "Were you trying to hurt me by letting me hear all that?"

She raises an eyebrow, then tilts her head. "If you were eavesdropping, that's on you," she replies evenly. But then she surprises me by moving closer and critiquing my stance. She comes to stand beside me and demonstrates the martial art form again, getting me to mimic her stance, and raising up my elbow, firming my stance.

I think, in Lyssa's mind, what she did was not intended to hurt me, but to make me...*aware*. She wants me to understand the reality of my situation, the harsh truth that Hadria doesn't care about me as a person, only as a prize in her game with Nero.

"Thank you," I say quietly, meeting Lyssa's gaze. "I needed that." And I don't only mean the correction to my form.

She seems to understand, giving a curt nod before standing back to watch me practice the movements she showed me. And I find myself grateful for Lyssa's lesson. It's a harsh truth to swallow, but it will make me stronger in the end.

"Lyssa," I pant out, "why do people call you the Wolf?"

She smiles a little. "Because they know I'll rip their fucking throats out given half the chance."

"And the others? Tony the Taxman? What's that about?"

At that, she gives an outright laugh. "Tony's known for taking limbs first as a warning if someone won't pay a debt, then lives if they still won't pay. So people started to advise others to 'pay the taxman,' which he found hilarious."

I'm not sure I do.

After that, I learn that Ilona the Impaler likes to use knives and other bladed weapons—and since she's of Romanian heritage, some humorist once described her as Vlad the Impaler's descendent, and the name stuck.

"And Ricky?" I ask. "His hands..."

Lyssa stops smiling. "Ricky was once tortured by a cartel, when they were trying to find out Hades' true identity. He lost seven fingers that day. And he kept his damn mouth shut. So you just think about that during this next meeting with Nero, Suzy. Think about whether you'd prefer to be here in Elysium with Hadria, or having your fingers severed in a dark room somewhere."

I stop dead, staring at her. "I thought you didn't want me here."

"I never said that." She stands from where she was leaning casually against a weights machine and heads toward the door.

"Make sure you keep going through those forms," she throws over her shoulder. "God knows you need all the practice you can get."

I think about Ricky Half-hands' lost fingers, and I do what Lyssa said: I keep practicing. And as I go through my forms, I make a silent vow to myself.

I won't ever forget again that Hadria doesn't see me as a person. That she sees me only as a weapon in her arsenal, a tool to use against her enemies.

And someday, I'll make her realize just how foolish she was to underestimate me.

CHAPTER 19

Hadria

WITH THE MEETING with Nero coming up quickly, I've tightened security to the highest levels across all my operations. Everywhere I go, Lyssa and two other handpicked bodyguards flank me, hypervigilant for any sign of danger. I know Nero will be looking for a chance to strike before the meeting, hoping to gain any advantage he can in this high-stakes standoff between us.

But I didn't get where I am by being unprepared.

One night, as I oversee our final security plans for the meeting Nero has proposed on his turf—my father will not be there, he tells me, which irks me a little, but is also very suggestive—I spot Aurora across the war room, watching me with that mix of curiosity and caution she always has. She must have slipped in at some stage. Since her first glimpse into the Syndicate's inner workings, she seems torn between fascination with my world and lingering unease.

I flag Lyssa and nod to where Aurora stands near the door.

"Remind Aurora that she'll be coming to this meeting with Nero. I want him to see her there."

Lyssa doesn't immediately react. After a moment, she says in a low voice, "You're a hundred percent sure about this, Boss? Could get messy."

"Then she should see the mess. She's with me now, like it or not. If nothing else, it will show her how good she has it here."

Lyssa shrugs. "Your call." She strides over to Aurora, delivering the news. Aurora gives a determined nod, glancing shyly my way. Lyssa claps her shoulder before returning to my side, a wry smile twisting her lips.

"Kid's low-key excited. Eager to prove herself to you, I'd say. Better watch she doesn't do something stupid."

I just grunt in response, keeping my gaze fixed ahead. But privately, I feel a spark of anticipation at having Aurora witness my power play with Nero firsthand. She'll see just what kind of world she's now part of.

And she'll see how well I treat her.

Speaking of which...

"I think she'd better have something new to wear," I say to Lyssa. Within minutes, we're loaded into one of my armored town cars, bodyguards watchful as we cruise towards one of the most exclusive boutiques in Chicago, which has opened at midnight on my personal request. The staff scramble to serve us, well-trained enough to ignore the presence of my entourage. I immediately take charge, selecting outfits I think will appeal to Nero's more base instincts.

I need him rattled, off-balance. If flashing Aurora's assets does that, so be it.

The personal shopper brings out my chosen selection, and then Aurora heads into the dressing room. Each time she comes out to show me an outfit, I circle her like a panther. And each dress makes her even more tempting than the last.

The first is a liquid gold dress covered in intricate beading, the material clinging to every curve. It's daringly short, showing off her toned legs. Aurora stares at herself in the mirror and I can't tear my eyes away, imagining pinning her against the glass and sliding my hands between those silken thighs.

The next dress, in rich orange silk, has a plunging neckline that reveals the tempting swell of her breasts. I ache to press my lips to the exposed skin there, teasing soft sighs from her. When she turns, I see it's completely backless, held together by two thin straps.

"I feel so exposed," she murmurs, cheeks flushed.

"You look powerful," I counter. "Men would fall to their knees for a chance to worship at your feet."

And God knows, they wouldn't be the only ones.

The next is a cream dress made of gossamer lace that conceals and reveals in maddening contrasts. Aurora looks ethereal yet intensely sensual.

And I like that the color will remind Nero of her wedding dress.

But Aurora balks at it. "I'm not a piece of meat," she snaps with a tone very unlike her usual soft murmurs. Her cheeks are flushed, blue eyes flashing.

I feel an unfamiliar pang of guilt. "Aurora." I tip her chin up. "Remember how I told you Lyssa was better at fighting than me?"

She shrugs.

"We all of us have different talents—different powers. And as a Syndicate, we all benefit when people lean into those powers. *You* have power here, if you use it right. Your beauty can undermine Nero, make him lose control. That gives *me* an edge. I'm not asking you to wear something sexy because you're a decoration. I want you to wear it to use as a *weapon.*"

I can see her turning this over in her mind. Then she lifts her head, expression morphing into something bolder, more calculating. "But I'm good at shooting, too," she says bullishly.

"No one said your good looks were your only talent. But, by God," I say with a little sigh, "they certainly are the most obvious. Your skill with a gun? That's something to keep under wraps for now. Be strategic, Sunshine. Distract with your face so they don't see what you're doing with your hands."

She considers that, and then nods slowly. "That one," she says, pointing at one that I discarded as too modest for her to even try it on.

But when she comes out in the azure velvet mini-dress that makes her eyes glow, I see how wrong I was. The front is very high, skimming over her collar bones in a wide neckline, covering her entire torso. But when she turns around, the daringly low back reveals a hint of butt cleavage.

And when she glances over her shoulder at me, I suck in a breath. She's transformed into a siren who could bring strong men to ruin with a glance. When she sees the look on my face, she seems to shed her innocence, blossoming into a woman fully aware of the effect she has on those around her.

On *me*.

"You'll stop Nero in his tracks," I tell her.

She turns, her hand drifting up my arm.

"And what about you, Hadria? Will I make you lose control too?"

Her touch scorches my skin. This captivating, maddening creature might just undo me completely. The air seems to vanish from my lungs. I want to cradle that defiant face in my hands and—

I force myself to step back. "It's perfect," I tell her. "Meet me downstairs." And then I head out of the dressing room and down to the boutique floor below, where I lean against the wall, cursing internally.

Since when do I lose my composure over a pretty girl playing games? Get it together.

But on the drive back to Elysium, I can't stop sneaking

glances at Aurora, wondering exactly what is going on in that tricky little brain of hers. Lyssa has warned me she's clever, cleverer than I think her, and perhaps Lyssa is right...

But then she catches my eye and smiles, slow and tentative, and an answering heat blooms inside me. I'm dangerously close to throwing all caution aside and pinning her against this plush leather seat.

My cell phone trills, breaking the moment. Ilona's voice filters through when I answer, grateful for the distraction.

"Eyes on the Gentleman, Hades. Corner diner at West Jackson and Jefferson."

We're not far from there. Opportunity knocks.

I lower the privacy screen to speak to the driver. "Change of plans," I tell him, and give him the address. Lyssa, seated next to him in the front, gives me a hard look. I turn away to speak to Aurora. "Stay in the car when we arrive. The driver will watch you."

She nods, eyes bright with curiosity. My fierce, fearless captive. How far she's come.

We pull up to the 24-hour diner and I step out, the other cars with us coming to a rough halt as well. Lyssa and my bodyguards form a phalanx around me as I enter, and the few patrons inside gape and murmur at the sight of us, then stream out fast, sensing danger.

And there at the counter, just like Ilona said, sits Johnny "the Gentleman" de Luca, back to the door. But I can see him watching me in the mirror behind the counter, and he turns when I'm close and reaches for a napkin, wiping off his fingers as he regards me.

"Hello, there." I sit up at the counter with him. "I'm Hades. You might have heard of me."

"Indeed I have," he says with a warm smile. "And what brings you in here?"

"That's my line. We need to talk."

Johnny's eyes go behind me to Lyssa and my other body-guards, calculating. My pulse drums in anticipation.

I do so enjoy these little chats.

CHAPTER 20

Aurora

AS SOON AS Hadria and everyone else's attention is fixed on the man at the counter, I get out of the car, ignoring the shout of the driver, and slip into the diner, pulse quickening at this small act of defiance. Hadria ordered me to remain in the car, but the temptation to witness her in action is too great.

I need to see how the woman who claims to own me handles potential threats.

Lyssa stands just inside the entrance, scowling as she spots me. I freeze, wondering if she'll unceremoniously drag me back to the car. But she gives a subtle nod, eyes glinting with what might be amusement. I let out a breath, grateful for this allowance.

The diner has a retro interior—gleaming chrome counter-tops and red vinyl booths. It's empty of all other patrons now, except for the older man at the counter. He wears what looks like a very expensive gray suit. This must be Johnny the Gentle-man. He cuts neatly into a slice of pie with refined dignity, seemingly oblivious to the impending confrontation, and smiles again at Hadria.

I half expect Hadria to do something awful to him—like—

grab his fork and stick it through his eye? But all she does is flag down the waitress for a coffee. I creep a little closer, but neither of them is keeping their voices low. Even the waitress seems to know enough to disappear once she's poured out Hadria's coffee. So when Hadria says, "I heard a rumor you might be in town on special assignment," I hear her clearly.

Johnny smiles urbanely. "Oh, no. I'm retired now. Just here to reminisce and enjoy the atmosphere. I was born here, you know. My family moved to New York when I was a boy. I wanted to see the Windy City again in my retirement."

Hadria studies him, eyes narrowed. "Retirement must be dull for a man of your talents."

"It has its benefits," Johnny says easily. "More time for family and golf. But I'll admit, I do miss the thrill of the work sometimes." He takes a thoughtful sip of his coffee, eyes meeting Hadria's in a subtle challenge.

"Are you here to put a bullet in my head?" she asks coolly.

Johnny pauses, carefully laying down his fork. When he replies, his tone holds only polite curiosity. "Now why would I want to do something like that?"

Hadria's eyes narrow. "Nero Imperioli wants me out of the way, and he's not above hiring out."

Johnny sighs heavily, as if explaining something to a stubborn child. "I'm retired, as I said—a consultant at most, these days. I'm simply revisiting old haunts."

Hadria studies him, tense and alert. Her hands rest lightly on the counter, ready to strike if needed. "You expect me to believe this is just a nostalgic visit?"

"I don't expect you to believe anything. But it's the truth." Johnny gives a gentle, fatherly smile. "That said, if you're concerned about potential threats, perhaps you would benefit from a few more allies?"

Hadria stiffens. "What are you suggesting?"

"Merely that friends can sometimes provide protection hired

guns cannot, as I'm sure you know yourself. If you wished to discuss a mutually beneficial affiliation with Juno Bianchi, for example, I could arrange an introduction in New York. Powerful women should stick together, don't you think?"

In the mirror, I see something close to shock flicker across Hadria's face, quickly masked. "Juno Bianchi, you say?"

"The same."

After a moment, Hadria shrugs. "I have all the friends I need already. But I'll think about what you've said."

Johnny inclines his head graciously. "Please do. Now, if you'll excuse me, allow an old man to finish his pie in peace."

Hadria slides off the stool and tosses some bills onto the counter. "My treat," she says, then scribbles down something on a napkin. "Enjoy yourself while you're here, Mr. de Luca. But if you get bored during your vacation, drop by Elysium for a visit —this is the address." She slides the napkin to him. "I'm sure I can find something to keep you entertained."

Johnny inclines his head graciously. "I appreciate the hospitality."

As Hadria turns, she spies me lurking nearby. Her stormy eyes flash with momentary annoyance as she marches over and takes my arm. I expect a harsh reprimand, but as she guides me firmly out the door, I see grudging admiration in her face. My act of defiance has intrigued more than angered her.

And in turn, I marvel at Hadria's composure and control. I ache to embody her strength. Her self-assurance. Her control…

Especially when all I can do is tremble at the thought of the harsh words that are about to fly my way.

"I thought I told you to stay in the damn car. Johnny the Gentleman is a very dangerous man."

I open my mouth to explain, but the words evaporate under her thunderous expression. And then, to my surprise, her grip on my arm loosens slightly.

"Just…get in the car, Aurora."

Her tone is more weary than angry now. My compliance seems to defuse her temper. Once settled in the idling town car, doors closed, all she says is, "You shouldn't have left the vehicle." But her composure unnerves me more than fury might have.

"I know. I'm sorry." I fiddle with my seatbelt, struggling to explain myself. "I just...wanted to see what was going on. I won't do it again."

Hadria sighs. "Of course you will. Your curiosity will be the death of you." But her words lack heat. "Don't pull something like that when we're meeting Nero."

"I won't," I whisper, but she doesn't seem to hear me. "Hadria," I say after a moment.

"Mm?"

"Who's Juno Bianchi?"

There's a long pause, and Hadria stares out the window the whole time. I think she's not going to answer me, but at last she says, "She heads up the richest mob Family in New York."

So Hadria's actions here in Chicago have started to attract attention from important people, even out of state.

Interesting.

———

A few nights later, my hands tremble as I pull on the blue velvet dress I'm to wear to the meeting with Nero. The plunging back makes me feel exposed in my weakest place, like I have a target right between my shoulder blades, but as I stare at my reflection in the mirror I can't see any sign of self-consciousness. With the amount of makeup I've piled on—smoked-out eyes, contour and bronzer, and an enormous amount of mascara—it would be hard for my true self to show through.

Is Hadria right? *Is* there a kind of power just in the way I look? Or was she only flattering me, manipulating me into wearing this dress?

I stare hard again at my reflection, seeing not myself, but some other creature.

If I'm really going to play this part of the sexually desirable trophy, then I should probably go all-in. I hike up my skirt—not far, since it's already so short—and I roll down the panties I was wearing underneath.

I'm definitely all-in now. I'll have to be careful getting in and out of the car, for one thing.

When there's a knock at my door, I'm expecting Lyssa, so when Hadria strolls in, my mouth falls open.

"You look amazing," she says, but in this clinical way that makes me wonder if she actually means it. "Turn around."

I turn to face the mirror, keeping my eyes on her. The gold heels I'm wearing are ridiculously high, but I'm still a few inches shorter than her, and she easily passes her hands over my head. And then, around my neck, she fastens a diamond collar. It sparkles ominously, Hadria's insignia of the three-headed dog, now cast in gold, resting in the hollow of my throat.

"What is this?" I ask, reaching up with a frown.

"It will undermine Nero's composure," she tells me. And then she adds, "And it will help you remember who you belong to." Her eyes burn into mine with a strange, fierce possessiveness that both unnerves and thrills me.

Her hand skims down my back and I shiver at her touch, hating that my body betrays me. Hadria notices and smiles, just a tiny quirk of the lips, before turning away. "It's time," she calls back. "Come on, Sunny. Time to shine."

The drive to the meeting is tense, Hadria staring out the tinted window while I fidget nervously. Lyssa sits across from us, gun already in hand, the metal glinting dangerously.

I haven't felt like this since my wedding day…like a lamb being led to slaughter.

The meeting location is an abandoned warehouse deep in the industrial district. Hadria's men flank the building before we get out of the car, their assault rifles in hand. My ankles wobble as I step out of the car. Hadria offers her arm and I cling to it more out of need than gratitude.

Inside the warehouse, the space is dimly lit and sparse. A long table sits in the center, surrounded by hard-backed chairs. Men in dark suits turn to stare as we enter. Their eyes crawl over me, undressing what little clothing I have on. I resist the urge to cover myself.

Hadria's grip on my arm tightens. "Gentlemen," she greets them coolly. They look away, chastened. These must be Nero's men, Imperioli Family members.

A door slams open across the warehouse and Nero storms in, eyes searching for Hadria. But when his gaze falls on me, his eyes widen, especially as I turn toward Hadria in a submissive gesture, and let him glimpse my full naked back.

"What's the meaning of this?" he demands through gritted teeth. "Why is she here?"

Hadria's smile is vicious. "I wanted you to see what you'll never possess."

Nero clenches his fists, nostrils flaring. Hadria's plan is working—and almost straight away. He's losing control, giving in to desire and envy.

She can play him like a fiddle.

Hadria takes a seat at the head of the table, gesturing for me to sit beside her. The men arrange themselves around us. Nero sits opposite Hadria, glaring sullenly.

"Papa doesn't know you're here," she begins. It's not a question.

"The old fool is too soft," Nero says.

"Well," she says with a cold smile, "I believe we are beginning to find some common ground, little brother. Let's see if we can find a little more, shall we?" Hadria begins outlining her demands. The Syndicate members listen intently, nodding along, and the Imperioli men are paying close attention too...

except for their leader. Nero fidgets in his seat, struggling to keep his eyes on Hadria.

They keep darting back to me.

To my nipples, tight and obvious under the dress. And to Hadria's diamond collar around my throat.

Never to my face.

But as the talks go on, he's not the only one at the table who can't help looking at me. Despite myself, I feel a heady rush at being the center of attention. Hadria was right. I have power here, power that I've tried to avoid for most of my life. My father always dangled me in front of men like these, but I was never dressed like this. Never so obvious, designed to claim attention, to divert.

It's intoxicating.

And yet there is one person in the room who seems to find it very easy to ignore me completely. Hadria continues speaking without even a glance my way, until Nero interrupts brusquely. "You can't just seize what's mine," he spits out.

Hadria raises an eyebrow. "I already have."

The implied meaning makes Nero flush crimson. He grips the table, leaning forward menacingly.

"I should rip your collar off the bitch and fuck her over this goddamn table. That'd show you just who owns this city."

The room grows tense, men exchanging uneasy looks. Hadria remains unruffled.

"You're welcome to try, little brother," she replies mildly. "But it would not end well for you." Her eyes flash a warning that makes every Imperioli man at the table lean back a little, unwilling to be in the crossfire.

And Nero leans back too, scowling.

His reactions reveal how easily Hadria manipulates him. His fragile ego crumbles under her psychological tactics. The dynamics of power in this room revolve around perception, and Hadria is a master puppeteer.

A puppeteer who controls my strings as well.

So I do something that is perhaps unwise, but is a little gesture of defiance, a little power play of my own.

I catch Nero's eye, and I run my tongue seductively over my bottom lip.

Abruptly, he surges to his feet. "That woman belongs to me," he snarls, stabbing a finger at me. "And I'll goddamn take her back from you tonight."

He nods sharply at his men, but the Syndicate members are already pulling out their own guns.

A split-second later, chaos erupts, shouts and screams filling the air. Hadria shoves me down, hard, under the table, and I go easily, my heart pounding wildly.

I grab frantically for her, but she's had to dive to the side as bullets splinter the chair in which she was sitting. "Hadria!"

Bullets pepper the walls, and I have to duck my head to avoid shards of wood and glass. The Syndicate members scatter around the warehouse, shouting and shooting, except for Lyssa, who tackles Hadria to the ground a few feet away, shielding her body.

Fear and adrenaline surge through me. Is Hadria okay?

Mario crawls over to me; Lyssa has taken a few of the top trainees on this mission. I guess it's a baptism of fire. "Suzy!" he gasps. "You okay?"

"Yeah." And seeing Mario, remembering the time I managed to overpower him—me, little Suzy Sunshine, flattening someone built like him—gives me my courage back. Peeking out over the top of the table, I spot Hadria and Lyssa. They've scrambled to their feet, and they're shooting as they move for cover.

Oh, thank God. *Thank God.* She's alive and she's okay.

But then, across the warehouse floor, I see one of Nero's men taking aim at Hadria's unprotected back. Without thinking,

I lunge for Mario, grabbing the gun from his limp hand. He gapes at me, stunned.

And then, praying to anyone that might be listening, I fire at Nero's man. The shot catches him in the shoulder and he stumbles back with a howl, blood pooling fast beneath him. His gun clatters to the floor.

Everything slows. I can only hear my thundering pulse as I lower the gun with trembling hands. What have I done? I've shot a man, possibly killed him. Bile rises in my throat.

Yet part of me burns with vicious satisfaction at the sight of him writhing around on the ground.

In seconds, Hadria and Lyssa dispatch several more Imperioli men with lethal efficiency. The rest turn tail and run, Nero along with them.

Panting in the aftermath, Hadria scans the room before her gaze settles on me. I expect anger over my interference, but instead she looks…impressed.

"Well done, Sunshine," she says softly. Lyssa's eyes flick between us, but I can't read her face.

The sudden quiet is eerie. Groans emanate from the injured and dying. The surviving Syndicate members pick themselves off the floor.

Mario helps me to my feet with a new air of respect. I've really proven myself now. Shown my claws. No longer am I a passive captive hanger-on to the group…I'm *one* of them.

I've been blooded.

The realization is both terrifying and exhilarating.

Hadria strides over and lifts my chin gently. Her gray eyes pierce mine, filled with swirling emotion.

"You saved my life," she murmurs.

I shake my head weakly. "I just reacted without thinking…"

"No." Hadria's voice is firm. "You were brave. Well done."

My heart stutters at her words. Perhaps it would have been smarter to just escape completely in the carnage. But the thought of her pale corpse splayed on this filthy floor, her brilliant flame extinguished forever, fills me with such sharp and sudden anguish I can hardly breathe.

And she seems to notice, pulling me close. "Come on," she says softly. "Let's get out of here." We leave the warehouse together, Hadria's warm hand pressed against my lower back. And my panic bleeds away, replaced by a hunger that surprises me with its ferocity.

In the car, I huddle up closer than necessary to Hadria, who keeps her arm around me. But she exchanges a look with Lyssa, who seems grim.

"I hope that little experiment was worth it," Lyssa says. "You know he'll retaliate."

Hadria nods. "And we'll be ready." She presses her nose into my hair, inhaling, and a chill of anticipation runs through me, raising the hairs on my arms.

Lyssa tuts. "At least wait until we get home," she growls, settling back in her seat.

But Hadria's arm stays tight around me and her fingers stroke softly against my arm the whole way back to Elysium.

CHAPTER 21

Hadria

WHEN WE GET BACK to the house, Lyssa stalks off, but I don't let go of Aurora until she's safely back in her bedroom. She started shaking about halfway home when the adrenaline began to wear off and only now, in the privacy of her room, does she finally speak.

"Did I…did I kill that guy?" she stutters out.

"You winged him," I tell her. "Hitting a moving target is tricky. Next time, Sunshine. Next time, you'll nail it."

"Oh," she breathes out, and it takes a moment to register that she sounds relieved rather than disappointed.

And that I am, too. She's ventured far into the darkness, this little sunbeam, but her hands still remain clean of blood— metaphorically, anyway.

I stand there looking down into her face, almost unfamiliar under all that makeup, and I want so desperately to taste her that I know I need to leave the room. But when I take a step back, she takes a step forward. "Don't go," she says. So simply, not begging, just saying it, as though she already knows I won't.

I couldn't, not now, not if my life depended on it.

"I won't go," I tell her. I should. God knows I'll need to have the Syndicate regroup, debrief...

But those are fleeting thoughts that evaporate like smoke when I see the clear need in her eyes. She takes another step, so that her breasts brush against me under that soft blue velvet, and she reaches up a tentative hand to my face.

I don't move, though I want to touch her so badly my fingers are aching. I want to grab up that honey-blonde hair and pull her head back so that I can slide my tongue down her throat, hear her gasp out in shock and pleasure—

"You were amazing tonight," she says, a note of wonder in her tone.

"*You* were amazing tonight," I retort, and the next thing I know, I'm kissing her. Her lips open under mine eagerly, and she responds with the same fervor I'm giving her, pulling her body up against mine, one of her hands sliding into my hair and the other pressed between us, covering my heart.

And I stop thinking and just *act*, seize a handful of that soft, sweet-scented hair that feels like a cloud in my palm, pull her head back so I can taste her throat, run my tongue right down that smooth column. She gives a soft moan so erotic that my clit jolts as though in response to electric shock, and I find myself baring my teeth, about to mark her out as mine—

I stop with a superhuman effort and raise my head again. "I'm sorry," I hear myself saying. But Aurora looks up at me with a mixture of fear and desire in her eyes.

"Don't stop," she pleads. "I want you."

My heart is so loud in my own ears that she must be able to hear it, too. It's thumping harder than it has this whole night. But I must be gentle, I remind myself. She's a virgin. If this is her first time, I want her to remember it fondly—

I cup her face in my hands and brush my lips over hers softly, turning the kiss as calm as I can. There's a beast inside me that wants to devour her, to throw her down on the bed and eat that sweet little pussy until she's screaming…but I need to take it slow.

Or so I think, until Aurora, who has thrown her arms around my neck suddenly mumbles under my lips. "No," she says. "Don't do that…"

I stop at once, release her, and step back.

She blinks at me.

"I'm sorry if I—" I begin, but she gives a frustrated growl, a sound so surprising coming from her that I break off at once.

"No," she says again. "Don't kiss me like I'm breakable. Kiss me like you—like you want to—God, why are you being so *nice?*"

It's my turn to blink. "You don't want me…nice?"

"I want *you*. I want the *real* you. Please—show me—"

It's the way her fingers reach up to the diamond collar I put around her neck, those elegant fingers stroking my insignia, and I feel a corresponding ghost-touch tracing over my throbbing cunt.

I move forward, crowding her back toward the bed, and when her knees hit the edge I stop her, take that blue velvet dress in my hands and rip it from neck to waist, letting those gorgeous little tits bounce free.

I've been wondering all night what they look like under her dress, those tight nipples peaked and perky under the material. I had to make sure I didn't even look at her in that damn warehouse, lest I made it very fucking obvious to everyone how mesmerizing I found her.

But now I can look to my heart's content. Her breasts seem about the perfect size to fit in my palms, and I test that theory, taking a soft and warm handful of them. She gasps and then she melts, her head lolling to one side in a submissive pose that only deepens the hard pulse in my clit. I squeeze a little to test their weight, their supple softness, teasing her nipples hard with my thumbs until she moans again, arching her back, and I feel a surge of dominant pleasure at her response. "Do you like that, Sunshine?" I ask, my voice low and husky. "You like having these sweet little titties played with?"

A gorgeous pink flush colors her chest, and Aurora nods shyly, her eyes half-lidded—but I can see the desire burning in them. I lean down, my lips hovering just above her left nipple, and ask, "Do you think you'll like me sucking on them?"

She nods, biting her lip. I pinch her right nipple a little harder, making her wriggle against me, practically humping my thigh where it's pressed between her legs. "Answer me properly, Sunshine, or it'll be a long time before you get what you want."

She summons up her courage, her voice still catching in her throat as she says, "Yes, please, Hadria. I'd like you to—to suck on them, please."

With a satisfied hum, I flick the sensitive nub with my tongue before closing my lips around it, sucking hard enough to make her moan. "Yeah," I say, letting it pop back out of my lips. "You definitely like that. What else do you like, I wonder?"

I have her pinned upright between me and the bed, but I want her fully naked and fully soaked before I lay her down on it. I take the ruined dress, hanging at her waist, and rip it completely off her so that all she's wearing is—oh, God, all she's wearing are those strappy gold heels that she can barely walk in, but that make her legs look endlessly long, and the diamond collar around her throat.

"You naughty little girl," I breathe, running a hand down her belly, stopping just before I get to the light dusting of curls. "What happened to your panties?"

She squirms, trying to press her pussy into my hand, but I grab her by the hips and still her so that I can get a good look. She's shining in the low light, her juices coating her swelling, pouting folds in a clear, tantalizing request for attention. "Tell me, Sunshine. What happened to your panties?" I ask again, my voice low and dangerous.

"I...didn't wear any," she whispers, her cheeks flushed a deep rose. "You told me to lean into my power, so I thought..."

"You thought you'd just let everyone smell this sugary treat?" I prompt, tracing down the soaking slit of her entrance with a fingertip, making her gasp and writhe against me. "I can smell you right now," I tell her, my lips against her ear. "Sweet honey. I bet you're delicious, Sunshine. Have you ever tasted yourself? Petted your kitty and then licked your fingers clean after?"

She lets out a cry of surprise, as though I've just guessed her deepest, darkest secret, and a tenderness rises up in me along with the need.

"I want to suck all that honey out of you, drink you in until you're begging me to stop. And then I want to soak my fingers in your juice and slide them into your mouth so you can see if it tastes as good as you remember. I'll fuck you until you explode again, sucking on your own cum."

I have to pass an arm around her waist as her knees buckle. "Please," she begs, her voice shaking. "Please, yes, please—"

"Would you like that, Sunshine? Would you like me to eat you all up?"

"God, yes," she groans, rocking against my palm now. I can feel how wet she is, how hot, how *needy*.

"Good girl," I praise her, and then I shove her back on the bed. She bounces, giggling in surprise, those gorgeous tits shaking, and leans up on her elbows, her shyness disappearing as desire takes over. "Show me where you want me." She opens her legs, tipping her hips up, and I get my first good look at her, her velvet pussy glistening in invitation.

I wanted to draw it out more, have her delirious before I even went near her, but her lips part as she shifts on the bed, and I see her hard, rosy clit standing up, begging for attention. I can't resist her any longer, so radiant and so wet and smelling so divine. So I dive in, give her a long, flat, hard lick up her whole length, from her neat little asshole, over her wet entrance, up to her clit and then back down again. She tenses up, her whole body taut as a bow, and then she collapses flat on the bed with a long, low groan.

"You taste even better than I thought you would," I tell her, tracing her slit with my tongue again. "Sunshine nectar, the sweetest thing on Earth."

"Hadria," she whimpers, "I'm so close already, please—!"

I pinch her clit in between my lips and flick it with my tongue, and she cries out, her hands gripping the sheets so hard I'm amazed they don't tear. Her hips buck, but I hold her in place, licking her like a delectable ice cream cone, sucking and lapping, teasing and devouring until her hips begin to move in time with my tongue, grinding herself against me as I eat her out.

"That's it," I coax her, "let go. Show me how much you want to come."

She's so far gone she can only mewl in response. *I* did this to her, I think with satisfaction, looking up at her writhing body. I brought her to this quivering mess and I could have her begging for more if I wanted. So I double my efforts, scraping my teeth gently against her clit before lapping up the fresh spill of arousal that rewards me for my efforts.

"You're so fucking delicious, I could eat you all night long," I tell her, my lips moving against her soaked, swollen sex.

She laughs, a hiccup of a laugh, and I dive back in, sucking her clit deep into my mouth and flicking it with my tongue until her warm thighs are clamped around my head, her body tight and tense. I give one last lashing of that tight little bundle of nerves with my tongue, and it's like I've detonated a bomb in her. Her whole body arches as she cries out, hips bucking off the bed, pushing hard against my face as she shatters, choking out my name.

I don't let up, wanting to draw every last drop of that delicious nectar from her before I'm finally sated. Finally, I ease up, staring up at her flushed, sweat-soaked face. "You taste even better than you look," I tell her as I crawl up her body. "And that's saying something."

She can only look at me, a dazed expression on her face, as I straddle her hips and draw a hand over her slick folds, making her shudder. I lick my fingers with an exaggerated hum of pleasure, making a show of it for her, rolling the taste of her around on my tongue like fine wine. "But you remember what I told you I wanted to do...right?" I swipe my fingers up her wet center once again, and her mouth opens in invitation.

I push my soaked fingers into her mouth and her tongue swirls around, eyelids fluttering shut as she tastes herself. When I pull them back, she gives a protesting squeak, until she realizes that I'm stripping off too, throwing my clothes aside as fast as I can, one hand on her pussy still, keeping her wet and warm and ready for me.

"I want you to come again, Sunshine," I tell her. "I want to ride you while you do, feel that hot little pussy explode under mine."

She moans, and I could come myself just from the desperate way she whimpers my name. I can't tease her any longer; I don't think I'd survive it if I did. I line up my aching cunt over hers and lower myself down onto her, making sure she's got enough pressure right over that swollen pink clit. Her hands grip my hips, nails digging into my skin as our clits catch together, sending sparks of pleasure through me, though she hisses between her teeth.

"You're sensitive," I breathe.

She nods. "Keep going, though," she pants out. "Please. Make it...make it hurt a little..."

"You like a little pain with your pleasure, hm?" I grind down on her, making her let out a small squeal. "Good girl. You can take it, can't you?"

In response, she shoves back up against me, making both of us moan as we grind together, wet and hot. My clit feels hard enough to cut her, and there's that darkness in me again that makes me want to tear her apart just to put her back together again. "That's right," I hiss out. "Show me what you're made of, Sunshine—"

Her nails dig into my hips, and I increase the pace, grinding harder, faster, reveling in the way her eyes squeeze shut and her mouth falls open in a wordless groan, so that I can't resist sliding my fingers in there again, pressing down her tongue. She sucks and moans, seeking out every atom of her flavor, and I fuck her harder as a reward, my cunt swelling on top of hers as I ride her without mercy, pulling little grunts and squeaks out of her. Her eyes squeeze shut, so I give her a smack on her thigh, just to the edge of painful, making them fly open, dazed and unfocused, but with the same fire I've come to expect from her.

"Look at me while you come," I growl. "I want to watch you fall apart for me." I reach up, take a handful of her hair again, and tug—not as hard as the beast inside me wants to, but hard enough for her to damn well feel it, and that seems to be all she needed; she bites down on my fingers in her mouth unthink- ingly, a long whine bursting out of her as she shakes and shud- ders in release.

And I'm done, too. I ride out my orgasm on top of her, our slick bodies slamming together as I come harder than I've ever come with anyone else, and when I bite her shoulder to muffle my screams, I can feel the bruise forming against my teeth.

"Hadria," she gasps out as I collapse on top of her, trying to catch my breath. "Oh, Hadria..."

I go rigid against her one last time, as hearing her say my name like that provokes another wave of almost-painful plea- sure, radiating out from my clit through my whole body. And then I remember myself and roll off her so she can breathe properly. She turns to me at once, snuggling into my side, and I feel her hot panting against my damp neck. I pull her close, tight and safe, and press my mouth to her forehead in a soft kiss.

Oh, God.

What have I done?

CHAPTER 22

Aurora

THE SOFT GLOW of the moon settles over the garden as I wander between the flower beds, not long before dusk. The blooms seem to come alive, their exotic aromas and vibrant hues a stark contrast to the darkness. For a brief moment, I can almost pretend I'm back in my childhood garden, a place that offered fleeting escape from the grim realities of my home life.

I kneel beside a flowering vine, its wispy blossoms curled tightly shut, preparing early on for the new day. My fingers brush the velvety petals as I'm flooded with bittersweet nostalgia. How many times as a child did I sneak into our tiny backyard to whisper secret wishes into the soft soil? It was an innocent ritual born of desperation. I believed somehow the earth would hear my pleas and deliver my mother and me from my father's volatile temper.

Those childish wishes never came true. My life only grew darker and more dangerous, culminating in my father callously selling me off to pay his debts. And yet, here I am, plucked from one precarious situation and trapped in another. No longer a naive child, but a woman—and yet still held captive, this time by the cryptic and commanding Hadria.

And after yesterday, I'm not sure I even *want* to escape anymore.

My hands give a sudden tremble as a memory flashes into my mind, and I can't stop the little moan that escapes me. Last night, Hadria Imperioli had her mouth between my legs, making me feel things I'd never felt before.

In the heat of the moment, I would have done anything for her. She seized control because I asked her to, stripped me bare —and not just of my clothes. I felt powerless, but not in a way that I disliked. Because I also felt profoundly *seen* by her. And the lines between us blurred, awakening a disorienting mix of resentment, arousal, pure lust...

And something else I dare not name.

Her body pressed to mine, her hands roaming possessively across my bare skin... My body sings with remembered pleasure, even as I hate my heart for being so easily swayed. I remind myself fiercely of my vow made just days ago: to always remember that, in Hadria's eyes, I'm just a pawn.

The problem is, I didn't feel like a pawn or an object last night. I felt...

Oh, I felt...

But I'm startled as Hadria herself appears silently at the edge of the garden, her tall figure bathed in shadows. I gasp softly, feeling like a child whose furtive wishes have just been granted.

When I woke today, Hadria was gone from my bed, though her scent was still all over the sheets, and I rolled around in them for a long time, a throbbing need between my legs as I remembered what we'd done. But I didn't see her at all today, and I started to worry.

What if I'd done something wrong?

What if she hadn't enjoyed it?

What if...

Hadria offers a wry smile, seeming to read my thoughts as

she extends a bottle of red wine and two glasses. "Care for a nightcap?"

I accept the glass after she fills it, though wine has never been to my taste. Hadria sits on the little stone bench and drinks deeply while I stay on my knees in the dirt and take a small, polite sip. She seems on edge, that usually-ironclad control slipping a little. We drink in silence and she stares not at me but at the lush tangle of night blooms, until she's drained her glass.

I've barely had a few sips of mine when she pours herself another.

Then: "Walk with me," she says, holding out a hand to help me up from my knees.

We wander along the garden paths, glasses cradled in our hands, the heady perfume of the flowers combining with the red wine, enveloping us both. I sneak a glance at Hadria as we walk in silence. The hard lines of her face are softened, a furrow between her brows. She seems lost in her thoughts, and I don't want to break into them.

I'm afraid of what they might be.

We turn back at last, heading once more into the night garden, where Hadria stops. And sighs.

"You seem a little…troubled," I venture cautiously. "Is it—did I do something—" I break off.

Hadria blinks as though she's forgotten my presence, and shakes her head with a smile. "Oh, no, little sunbeam. You're completely perfect. That's the…" She trails off with a sigh and takes a slow sip of wine before answering. "Do you resent being here?"

Her blunt question startles me. "At first I did. But now…it's more complicated than that."

Hadria nods slowly, processing my words. "What happened between us last night," she says, choosing her words with care, "I think it shouldn't have happened."

"Was I very awful?" I ask, cringing.

She stares at me for a long moment. "You were...absolutely wonderful, Aurora. And I hope you don't regret what happened."

"Oh, no," I say at once. "No, definitely not."

"But you are still a captive here," she goes on gently. "And captive by necessity. I know you want more freedom, more agency in your life. You told me that yourself when you begged me to teach you to defend yourself."

I swallow and think about how to respond to that. "Can you blame me?" I ask her at last. "Even pet birds will fly away if you leave the cage open."

I'm getting too close to the truth with a comment like that, but Hadria just drinks from her glass again. "But I can't let you go," she says at last. "I thought about it. Last night, when we were...I thought about it then. Opening that cage door and letting you decide your own fate. But I can't do that, Aurora."

"I know," I say mechanically. "I'm proof of your victory over Nero."

She shakes her head. "It's not that at all, Sunshine. No. If I let you go, you wouldn't be *safe*. There's nowhere you could go on your own that Nero wouldn't find you, and when he does...he would do terrible things to you, in order to punish *me*."

She's right. I can see that. I stare back at her, and then I ask the question that's been haunting me since I left her bed. "Do I mean anything more to you than a symbolic victory? Because if not, the easiest solution would be to kill me."

"Don't," she says sharply. "Don't *ever* say things like that. I would never..." She trails off. "No, Sunshine. You're much more than a symbol to me. You've unsettled me. There's something about you—" She steps closer. "I'm not afraid of anyone. But I'm a little afraid of *you*."

My breath catches. Slowly, deliberately, she takes my glass from me and sets both mine and hers aside. The air between us grows charged as she brushes a lock of my hair behind my ear, her wine-stained lips hovering an inch from mine in silent question.

In answer, I slide my fingers through her dark hair and bring her mouth down to mine.

CHAPTER 23

Aurora

HADRIA'S KISS is soft and teasing, but it awakens the same driving need in me as last night, an overwhelming desire to *submit* to her.

And I feel a faint wave of disgust with myself, that all those hopes and dreams I had to escape could be wiped away with a single kiss from the woman who keeps me captive...

But I can't feel resentful for long. When her hands slide over me, they're careful, questioning, making sure I want what she's offering. She whispers in my ear, asking outright what I want, what I need from her—

"I want you," I murmur. It's the truth, God help me. I want *her*. I want my freedom, but I want Hadria, too, and I'm terrified that they're not compatible.

"I want you too, little sunbeam," she tells me, tipping my face up. "I'd like to taste your sweetness again. Should we go back to the house?"

I grin. "Nope."

Her eyebrows go up. "Right here?"

"Well—maybe over here," I say, taking her hand and leading her to a more secluded part of the night garden, where a patch of soft grass is hidden by the trailing fingers of a small willow tree. I sweep aside the swinging tendrils like a curtain, and Hadria smirks.

"Cozy," she remarks—and then strips off her jacket and lays it out on the ground in a move so chivalrous I feel my heart flutter.

"Um, thanks," I say awkwardly, and she helps me lie down on top of it, then joins me, pulling me into her arms.

For a minute we just lie there, staring up at the stars through the willow tree branches. Hadria's hand strokes my arm softly, and she shifts me a little so she can see into my face. "Last night was intense," she murmurs.

"I like intense," I say at once. I'm already throbbing between the legs, almost shocked at how immediately wanton I feel.

"I like it, too," she replies. "But there are other ways to be intense. Would you like me to show you?"

Would I like her to show me? I'd like her to rip my damn clothes off and fuck me, that's what I'd like. But I just say, "Yes, please."

She tips my face up with a finger under my chin and begins to kiss me again, taking her time, savoring the taste of my lips, the way our mouths fit together. I moan softly into her mouth, my body already on fire for more. But she stays slow, agonizingly slow, trailing her lips down my jawline, flicking her tongue against my earlobe, her fingers rubbing a soft, teasing arc over my breasts. I arch up against her with need, wanting more, *needing* more.

"Easy," she murmurs, nipping at my neck playfully before soothing the sting with her tongue. "I want to enjoy this. I want you melting into a puddle before I even think about getting you off."

I groan in frustration. "I'm already halfway there!"

She chuckles against my skin. "The best part of any meal is the anticipation," she purrs in my ear. I'm going to protest again, but then her hand slides down my stomach and into my pants, stroking gently through my curls. "Good kitty," she murmurs.

I'm already so wet, so ready for her. Her fingertip slides down my soaking seam, and I open my legs wider, let my lips part of their own accord, hoping that her fingers will brush against my clit.

"You're so hot for me," she says into my hair. "Burning up. A little furnace." And she gives me what I'm so desperate for at last, a soft pass over my clit that leaves me writhing, pleading. "That feel good?" She strokes me a little firmer, then takes my clit in two fingers, cradling it gently. The sensation is exquisite, and I arch into her touch, moaning without thought for who might overhear.

"Yes, I think you like that," she chuckles. Her free hand slides up my shirt and captures my breast, squeezing gently. Pleasure rockets through me, a white-hot line from my nipple to between my legs.

"Oh, Hadria," I moan, unable to hide the want in my voice. "Please, please—I need more."

But she slows down, nibbling at my collarbone. "Impatient little sunbeam," she teases. "We have all night." She draws out the moments, tapping at my clit softly with her fingertips while she pinches and releases my nipple over and over again, and it's maddening and blissful all at once. I'm squirming underneath her ministrations, desperate for more, relishing my body's own capacity to surprise me.

Because it's never felt so good before. I've touched myself, of course, brought myself to what I thought was a peak...but it was never, ever like the sensations Hadria brought out in me last night. The sensations she's bringing out in me now...

I moan as she rubs a little harder. "That's it," she croons. "Let me hear you. God, you're incredible. So responsive..." She kisses me again, tongue delving into my mouth as her fingers work their magic beneath my clothes, and I whimper into her mouth.

I wish I could see her face—but then she pulls back and looks down at me, eyes blazing, and her hand withdraws from my panties.

I make a noise of protest, but then I realize what she's doing —she takes my hand and guides it to her waistband, waiting patiently as I fumble with the buttons, then gracelessly shove into her underwear. "Like this," she tells me, when I look up to her face uncertainly, and she slides her hand back down between my legs, stroking me. "Go on," she prompts, and I try to match her movements. It takes me a few minutes to really get the hang of it, but I do at last—I can tell from the way Hadria's breath hitches, the way she grinds herself against my hand. "Oh, good girl, Aurora," she pants, "you're a natural."

I feel a surge of pride at her praise, and I kiss her, fierce and possessive. It's my turn to take control, though I don't know how long I can keep it up when she feels so good between my fingers, when *her* fingers are driving me crazy, when her tongue is teasing mine like that. Overwhelmed by the sensations, I break the kiss and tug open her shirt so I can taste her skin. She tastes just like her spicy scent suggests, and in combination with the heady night blooms around us, I think...

I think I'm a little *high*.

"You're going to make me come," she sighs, and that just makes me redouble my efforts. There's something so intoxicating about being in control of her pleasure, watching her face soften with desire as my fingers dance against her—and then she lets out a long hiss, back arching, her own fingers stilling on me.

I did it. I *did* it, I made her—

But then she reminds me who's *really* in control here, as she tugs my hand out of her pants and pushes me onto my back. "That was very well done, Sunshine," she says as she looks down at me, a devilish grin on her full lips. "But now it's my turn. And I think it's time to turn up the intensity." And she slides a finger into me, gently, letting me adjust to the sensation, before she pulls it out slowly. She pushes in again and I give a moan as she does. I never knew it could feel so good to have something *inside*, something to clench hold of while her thumb plays with my clit.

"Good?" she asks.

"Good," I manage to pant out.

She was right—somehow, this is just as intense as last night, even though it's much slower...much more tender. I wrap one leg around her hips, drawing her closer, wordlessly pleading for more. To my relief, Hadria obliges, sliding another finger into my wet heat and curling them a little, until I'm shaking with the sensation. She seems to know my body as well as her own, as if she can read my mind and knows exactly where to touch me, how to make me moan for her, how to make me come for her. Because I'm going to, I can feel it, the coil of need tightening inside me again, but different to the frantic need of last night. This is...thicker, more potent, like I have molten gold bubbling around inside me. The tension builds, fed by every thrust of her fingers, every circle of her thumb. The world around us fades away, and there's only her touch, her scent, her presence.

"Let go for me, Aurora."

It's as if her words are the permission I've been waiting for. I *do* let go, crying out as my climax rushes through me in wave after wave of tingly heat. My back arches off the ground, and I clutch hard at the grass around me, head thrown back as Hadria's name spills from my lips. She keeps working her magic, prolonging my pleasure, until at last I collapse, panting and spent.

I give a whimper of protest when she finally pulls her fingers out of me, but she only chuckles and pulls me close again.

"Well," she sighs happily. "I haven't had fun like that for a *long* time."

I nestle closer against her strong frame. "Not even with Lyssa?" I ask before I can stop myself.

Hadria gives a startled laugh. "*God*, no. Lyssa is like a sister to me, we could never..." She shakes her head, still chuckling. "Besides, she has a very specific type, and I am *not* it. No. Definitely not."

Her admission sends a spike of satisfaction through me. I trail light kisses along her elegant collarbone as she continues stroking my hair.

At last Hadria speaks again, her voice low and throaty. "Come to the Syndicate meeting tomorrow night, so that I brag to them all about your heroics last night. Will you do that? Because I think it's time you took a seat at the table, Aurora."

I tense, the heady languor fleeing my limbs. Just a few days ago, knowing that I'd earned Hadria's trust enough to sit at the table in the war room would have filled me with a sense of victory. I'd be a step closer to freedom, or so I would have thought.

And I would have been wrong. I see that now. Hadria is right; without protection, I'll only fall back into Nero's hands, and he makes me shudder for all the *wrong* reasons.

Whereas Hadria...

Sensing my unease, Hadria tips my chin up to meet her eyes. "You've more than proven yourself," she says, assuming I'm concerned about her offer of a seat at the table. "No one would dare question your right to be there."

"I'd be honored," I tell her. It's the right answer, judging by her smile.

"And this thing between us," she says, then hesitates. "We should keep it quiet. I don't want Nero to have any more reason to punish you for my actions."

She's the one who flaunted me in front of him, but I don't point that out. I just nod.

"Not even Lyssa," she says, as she unwraps her arms from me. "You understand?"

I'm pretty sure Lyssa already suspects, given the way Hadria held me close in the car on the way back from the meeting...but again, I just nod.

We get up then, Hadria helping me rearrange my clothes, and I shake out her jacket. "I hope we didn't stain it," I say.

"I hope we did." Hadria gathers the discarded wine bottle and glasses as we go back into the open area of the night garden. "Why does Lyssa call you Suzy?"

I laugh, surprised. "It's just a nickname. Suzy Sunshine. At first it was an insult, but now..." I give a little shrug, a half-embarrassed smile. "Everyone calls me Suzy. The trainees. Even Mrs. Graves, sometimes."

Hadria gives a sniff. "You have a perfectly good name in Aurora. Still..." She brushes a chaste kiss to my forehead. "It's true, you've brought a little sunshine into Elysium."

"Hadria," I say quickly, catching her hand before she turns away, "may I ask for something?"

"Anything."

"My mother...I'd like to see her again. Please."

She thinks for only a moment before nodding. "I did say she would be allowed to visit. Not your father, mind—and if Sylvia thinks she can bring him along again—"

"She won't," I say, though I have no idea at all whether she will. But I don't think it was her decision to bring him along last time, either. "Thank you," I add, and press a kiss to the palm of her hand, the scent of my own excitement still faintly on it.

Hadria's other hand strokes over my hair, and then she's gone, a lithe shadow disappearing into the night. Alone once more, I sink back into the cool grass and bring my hands to my face, inhaling Hadria's scent now, trapped on my skin again.

And doubt winds its thorny vines around my heart.

This fragile thing blooming between us is undeniable. And

part of me wants to give into it, to stay here, a princess locked away in a tower, and enjoy all the things that Elysium—that Hadria—has to offer.

But that part of me is the *old* part, the weak little girl who shrunk away from any conflict. I've changed in my time here. I can fight, now. I can shoot.

I can kill...probably. If I have to.

But my heart isn't yet the stone I wish it was. I still have more work to do—more plans to make—if I'm going to snatch my freedom for myself.

And maybe my mother can help.

CHAPTER 24

Hadria

THE NEXT NIGHT, I sit enthroned in my chair on the raised dais at the far end of the war room. I'm early tonight, alone before anyone arrives, and I stare unseeing at the heavy oak table. My thoughts drift to Aurora, as they so often do these days.

How completely things have changed between us, in ways I could not have predicted when I first brought her here. That day she was a trembling fawn dragged away by a lion. Now she walks the corridors and grounds of Elysium with her head held high.

Yes, she's come a long way from the delicate, wraith-like girl I first laid eyes on in her parents' living room. And I've fulfilled my promise to her, to strengthen her, to remake her.

So why does her transformation fill me with disquiet?

Last night in the garden, I noticed again the hollows under her eyes that no amount of rest seems able to banish. She still takes delicate bites of her meals, as though her stomach has shrunk too small to want full nourishment. Her skin has lost the radiant glow it held when first she came here. She's still beautiful, but it's a colder beauty now, pale and remote as the moon.

Not so sunny these days.

But she's everything I aimed to shape her into, so why does victory feel so hollow?

"Well, if it isn't my favorite crime lord brooding on her throne," drawls a familiar voice, and I look up to see that Lyssa is standing there at the foot of the dais, an insolent grin on her lips. There are very few who would dare approach me with such casual irreverence, but Lyssa knows damn well she will always get away with it.

"What's got you frowning like that?" she goes on, leaning on the arm of my chair. "You'll scare all the new recruits away if you keep making that face."

I raise an eyebrow. "I wasn't aware I employed so many cowards. Perhaps I should reconsider their positions."

"Oh come on, don't be like that." She wanders down to the table and hops up on the edge of it, ignoring my glare. "I'm just saying you've seemed...distracted lately. Distracted and conflicted. Very unlike the Hades I know."

"I don't know what you're talking about," I say dismissively. "I'm focused on the work, as I always am."

"Mmhmm." Lyssa fishes a switchblade from her pocket and begins casually cleaning her nails with it. "This wouldn't have anything to do with a certain captive turned protégé, would it?"

"Aurora is an asset, nothing more. Her contributions to the Syndicate's operations have proven useful, that's all. And she saved my damn life, Lyssa. I won't forget that in a hurry."

"An asset." Lyssa repeats my first words skeptically. "So those drippy looks I've seen you giving her, the private meetings in the garden...that's all just business, is it?"

"Watch it, Wolf." My voice holds warning. "You're taking too many liberties."

She holds up her hands placatingly, but her gaze remains knowing. "Come on, Hades. I'm only speaking out of concern. For both of you, actually."

I frown, torn between annoyance and surprise. Lyssa has never shown much interest in my affairs before. But she seems to read my silence as permission to continue.

"You care for the girl. I've known you a long time, and I've never seen you look at anyone the way you look at her. But—" She leans forward and fixes me with serious eyes. "—this life will eat her alive. Whatever it is you feel, you need to stamp it out—for *her* sake."

"If your training is insufficient—"

"It's not my training," she says, ignoring the implied insult. "She's got a natural talent with marksmanship and she's not terrible at hand-to-hand—I mean, she's not good, but she could probably surprise someone long enough to run away from them. But she shouldn't *have* to live like that. That's my point. She's an innocent, and keeping her here is only going to destroy that innocence."

Aurora's wan face floats before my mind's eye once more. Lyssa always had an uncanny talent for seeing to the heart of things, and it's only what I've been thinking about myself tonight. Aurora has changed so much, learned *too* well. What sweet traits of hers have been lost to the shadows forever?

I feel a sudden ache in my chest.

"What do you expect me to do?" I ask coldly. "I can't just throw her out on the streets. Nero would snatch her in an instant—"

"Of course he would, and I'm not suggesting that," Lyssa sighs. "I'm just saying…she needs more than a little midnight gardening to cling to what's left of who she was. Let her have the days, too. The sunlight, the flowers, time away from *this*." She gestures around the windowless war room. "It's the only way to preserve what makes her…*her*."

The thought of allowing Aurora loose in the day spikes alarm. Since I brought her here, I've controlled when she wakes, what information she receives, who she interacts with. The thought of relinquishing any of that authority fills me with unease.

Outwardly, I keep my tone bored, dismissive. "Your concern for my prisoner is touching, but unnecessary. The girl knew what sort of world she was entering when she willingly decided to involve herself with the Syndicate. Any changes in her are of her own making—and thanks to your help, I might add."

Lyssa's eyes flash with a rare anger. "I've never known you to lie to yourself, Hadria. Suzy's had no choices but the ones forced on her—by her father, by Nero, and now by *you*. You took her from everything she knew, dropped her into a viper's nest, and now you're saying she spontaneously grew fangs on her own?"

I slam my hand down on the arm of my chair, unconsciously mimicking my father's favorite gesture. "Enough! She belongs to me, and I'll do what I want with her."

Lyssa presses her lips together, then nods. "As you say, Hades. I only want what's best for the Syndicate."

"And while we're on the subject, you and everyone else can stop calling her fucking *Suzy*."

I wish I hadn't added that. It makes me sound petty, vetoing a nickname. We all have them, after all, from Tony the Taxman to Ricky Half-hands, to *me*.

Hades.

I exhale, get myself back under control. Lyssa has always spoken her mind to me when no one else dares. I can't fault her for her honesty, misguided though it may be. "Let's focus on Nero," I tell her.

"Why don't we do that," she says neutrally, as the rest of my lieutenants start to file in.

It's only my lieutenants tonight, a top-tier meeting, and I'm grateful for that. I don't have the patience for the bullshit that inevitably comes with a full meeting of the Syndicate.

"What's the good news?" I ask, once they're all seated near the head of the table.

"There is none," Lyssa says bluntly. "But there's plenty of bad. Ricky?"

He doesn't want to speak, but he forces it out. "It seems some of our people have...defected, lured by Nero's promises of power."

I go very still. "Defected?" My voice is arctic. "They dare betray *me?*"

"Five soldiers," Ricky says grimly.

"All from Ricky's crews," Tony the Taxman adds. "The rest of us have a firmer hand on our people. No offense intended," he says with a smarmy smirk at Ricky's hands.

For a second, Tony and Ricky just look at each other. And then, with a snarl, Ricky launches himself across the table, fists flying hard enough to prove to Tony that he might be missing a few fingers, but he doesn't need them to kill a man.

I watch wearily as Lyssa intervenes, my mind still on those rats who abandoned me for Nero's service. The insult is intolerable. Once Lyssa—with Ilona's help—has dragged Tony and Ricky away from each other, I stare hard at Tony. "I expect my lieutenants to stand firm with each other, not to tear each other down. Make a crack like that again, and you'll find yourself without hands at all. Clear?"

Tony swallows. "Clear, Boss."

Then I turn to Ricky, who is still glaring at Tony. "As for you —you need to show me you can control your crews, or I will take them off you. And find those five soldiers who deserted us. When you locate them, make their ends slow and painful, and leave their corpses on display. I want them used as examples to any who would break faith with me."

Ricky nods. "Consider it done, Boss."

My anger has cooled entirely, shifting into calculation. With a reduced force, I'll need to adjust our strategies for seizing several contested territories from Nero's allies. Muscle alone won't win this war; we need to strike with precision.

I rise from my chair to sit beside Lyssa at the table, gesturing for my lieutenants to show me the maps and reports. For the next hour we're absorbed in an intricate dance of tactics and counter-tactics, reworking elements of our plans.

And for a time, I lose myself in the cold pleasure of strategy.

But as soon as my lieutenants have left the war room, I find my thoughts circling back to the moonlit garden, its vivid blossoms, and the woman who tends them. And I'm gripped by a strange feeling, foreign enough that it takes me a moment to place it.

Fear.

Fear that I'm losing something precious. That Aurora will change too much, that—as Lyssa said—she'll lose that thing that makes her *her*.

No matter how much I didn't want to hear it from Lyssa, I know my Wolf is right. It's inevitable; no one ever leaves Elysium the same as when they arrived. If I keep her here, Aurora will transform, and I might lose her completely in that process.

But I can't see a way to free her, either.

CHAPTER 25

Hadria

THE NEXT NIGHT I awaken slowly, as if rising from the depths of a dark sea, and I resist, because I'm dreaming of Aurora. But all too soon, the soft silk sheets glide over my skin, the lingering vestiges of the dream slip away. My eyes open to the familiar darkness of my chambers, lit only by the soft glow of the floor lamp in the sitting room outside, the outside shutters keeping out the late afternoon sun and the view of the grounds beyond.

I sit up at the gentle rap of knuckles on my door. But before I can call out to permit entry, the door opens, and she is there, tentative yet resolute, a tea service balanced precariously in her grasp.

Aurora.

Not Mrs. Graves.

"I'm sorry, I didn't mean to wake you." Aurora's voice is a strained whisper in the stillness. She hurriedly sets the tray down on the antique coffee table.

"You didn't. Is it time for breakfast already?"

Aurora glances at the clock. "Actually, you've...slept in, if that's the term for it. It's ten past midnight."

My brows rise in surprise. Slept in? Me? Aurora fidgets under my steady gaze, a rosy blush creeping across her cheeks.

"I persuaded Mrs. Graves to let me bring up your breakfast. Or is it supper?" she adds, a nervous laugh escaping her lips. Her eyes flit to the floor.

I study her intently, reading each nuance of expression, every minute movement. She's never entered these rooms unbidden. It's an uncharacteristic boldness.

And as for Mrs. Graves, she should damn well know better than to let anyone else into my rooms without my express permission. "Mrs. Graves is unwell?" I keep my tone even, not betraying the undercurrent of curiosity.

"Oh no, she's quite alright." A pause as Aurora weighs her next words carefully, mindful of my scrutinizing stare. "I...I just asked if I could be the one to bring you your meal tonight. I wanted to see you."

Aurora seems to have wrapped Mrs. Graves around her little finger as easily as she did me—and even Lyssa, who has *never* in her life suggested I go easier on someone, like she did last night with Aurora.

But Aurora's approach interests me. Our dynamic has shifted, a subtle realignment evident in her demeanor. The notions of captor and captive no longer hold true, if they ever really did.

Aurora occupies an undefined space, not quite prisoner, nor guest, nor lover...

But not quite *not* a lover.

I pat the side of my bed, gesturing for her to sit as I sit up myself, letting the sheets fall beneath my breasts, just to see her reaction.

She blushes. Sweet.

She perches tentatively on the edge of the bed and I feel my brows furrow as I look more closely at her. "You look concerned. Has something happened?"

"No," she says quickly. "But I…" She looks up at me from beneath her lashes. "I wondered if you'd thought about my request, to see my mother again."

"Oh, that." I yawn. "I already sent word to her, last night after I left the garden. I'm just waiting for a response."

Aurora's smile lights up her features. Impulsively, she reaches for my hand, giving it a gentle squeeze. I freeze at the unexpected contact, the simple gesture launching a riotous storm within me. She seems to sense the shift, pulling back.

And I instantly miss her touch.

"I should get up." My voice comes out hoarse. I gesture lamely at the tea service and Aurora stands quickly, removing the tray she just set over my lap. She does it without Mrs. Graves' finesse, so that the china rattles alarmingly, particularly when she sees that I'm completely naked.

"That will be all, Aurora." It comes out terser than I intended, but if she stays much longer I'll find myself kissing her, and…*so* much more. But Aurora just stands there, uncertainty shading her eyes. "It was a—a pleasant surprise to see you," I add, trying and failing to inject a note of warmth into my voice before escaping into the bathroom.

Her hurt look haunts me and the click of the lock only accentuates the silence. I brace myself against the vanity, steadying my suddenly unsteady legs. Foolish, foolish…I berate myself for the charged moment, for allowing her nearness to unravel me so easily. I avoid my reflection in the gilt mirror as I step into the shower, hoping the scalding water will re-center my scattered thoughts.

But it's no use. She permeates my thoughts, my dreams, my carefully cultivated walls thinning day by day.

I am losing myself, and I am terrified.

I shut off the shower abruptly, and glare at my foggy reflection in the mirror as I dry myself roughly. But when I emerge, wrapped in a silk robe, Aurora is still in my bedroom, seated on the bed, hands folded neatly in her lap.

She looks up as I enter, eyes wide. I halt dead. She rises slowly, but she says nothing.

"What do you want?" I ask eventually. "What do you want from me, Aurora?"

The desperation in my voice surprises me, and Aurora just worries at the hem of her sleeve. Finally, she raises her eyes tentatively to meet my own. "I want to ask you something."

I nod, not trusting myself to speak. Aurora takes a steadying breath.

"When you...when we're...together—" She clears her throat. "Does it mean anything to you?"

"Ah, Sunshine..." My voice shakes. I can't stop it. I close the distance between us before I can think better of it, taking her hands in mine. "It means far *too* much. That's the problem." I squeeze her hands gently. "I'm sorry if I've upset you. That was never, ever my intention."

Aurora lets out a shaky laugh, and her face reddens. "But then how can you be so cold toward me, after—after—"

Oh, God.

I reach up to cup her face. "I'm cold because...because that's who I *need* to be. It would be too dangerous for me to let anyone..." I trail off, cursing myself. There's an obvious end to that sentence, and I hope she doesn't find it.

"Into your heart?" she murmurs, and turns her head, pressing a feather-light kiss to my palm. My breath hitches. Slowly, cautiously, she guides my hands to her hips, her body molding against mine. "Then if not your heart...your bed?" Her request is scarcely a whisper.

I know I should pull away, put up my walls once more. Instead, I draw her closer still, fingers tangling in her hair as my lips find hers. She responds tentatively at first, then with growing fervor until my whole body is thrumming with the desperate *need* for her. There is no Syndicate, no threats beyond these walls, no expectations to uphold.

There is only her, only me, only the truth of what lies between us.

Aurora leads me toward my own bed, our kisses growing feverish. My hands roam her body as I push her back on the silk sheets and crawl over her, my lips blazing a trail down the column of her throat.

The way we make love tonight is different again to the previous two nights. This time, my touches walk the line between tender and intense. I'm attentive to each hitch of breath, every whispered plea, careful not to push too far, but I still indulge in my need to possess her completely as I make her beg for release, beg to my full satisfaction and then a little beyond, so that her orgasm, when it comes, has her screaming the damn house down.

But in the aftermath, limbs entwined and hearts still racing, my mind is unsettled once more. Without the haze of desire, doubts begin creeping back in, worries about this new precipice we're standing on.

My people must be wondering where I am, but no one dares disturb me. No doubt Mrs. Graves is refusing entry to anyone, since she must be very aware that Aurora is still with me. Well, business can wait. Haven't I earned a few hours of downtime? I push aside my worries as a lazy sense of satisfaction crawls over me, turning my limbs to liquid, until Aurora's soft voice pulls me back to the present.

"Can I ask you something?"

I stiffen slightly but keep my tone even. "Of course." Please, not something to ruin this perfection. Not now.

Aurora tilts her head up to meet my eyes. "Why do you try so hard to prove yourself to them?"

Confusion knits my brow. "Them?"

"Your family. Your father. After the way they've treated you, overlooked you...why do you still want their validation?"

I open my mouth, then close it again, stunned to silence. I try to summon the usual irritation at the mere mention of my father, but find none. Only a hollow sadness.

He gave up on me long, long ago. So Aurora's question is nothing but reasonable.

Why the hell do I care?

Why care about the Imperioli Family at all? I've built my own reputation, my own name, my own *empire*. I'm wealthier than Nero will ever be and I hold more influence than he ever will. Juno Bianchi is not likely to be interested in dealing with him, for example.

But she would with me, if I asked her to.

Aurora's eyes are knowing, yet kind.

"I don't know," I answer finally, truthfully. The clock strikes two, the sound reverberating through my rooms.

Aurora's hand finds mine beneath the sheets, anchoring me. "You're your own woman, Hadria. It seems to me that you owe them nothing."

I let her words settle over me, allowing myself to imagine, just for a moment, the possibility of a life unfettered by my family's shadow. Is it even possible, at this point?

Or am I damned to repeat the same destructive cycles, over and over?

CHAPTER 26

Aurora

THE DIM LIGHT filtering through from the sitting room casts shadows across Hadria's face as she lies next to me in her huge bed. Even in repose, her features maintain their sharp, aquiline beauty, though her typical guardedness has fallen away, replaced by a pensiveness I've seldom seen.

I came here tonight intending only to ask about my mother, but after seeing Hadria naked, that hot tingle ran all through me, and my legs simply refused to let me leave…

And now here we are, tangled up in each other, my body sated so deeply I don't think I've ever really known what it meant to be relaxed before.

My last comment, tentative yet bold, still hangs between us. *It seems to me you owe them nothing.* Over the past few months I've seen how fiercely Hadria guards herself, shrouding her inner world behind an impenetrable wall of ice. So I don't know how she'll take my observation. If she'll turn Ice Queen again and order me out of the room.

When she finally parts her lips, her voice is low, almost a murmur in the hushed room. "Respect. That's what I truly want.

Not just power, but respect. The kind of bone-deep awe commanded only by those born to lead." She pauses, gray eyes clouding with bitter memories. "As a child, I was denied that respect because of the circumstances of my birth. My father saw me as nothing but a disappointment from the moment I came into this world without a Y chromosome. When Nero was born, Papa spent a *fortune* announcing him to the world. So I vowed to seize with my own hands the position that should have been my birthright. To *make* my father acknowledge me." Her voice is cold and implacable. "To have him come to me on his knees, begging for scraps from the daughter he discarded."

The venom in her words sends a shiver through me. In silence, I reach for Hadria's hand, lacing our fingers together. After a taut moment, she relaxes into my touch, her cold fury settling back beneath the surface.

I speak gently. "But you've achieved so much already. You command an army that strikes fear across the city. And though your methods are...ruthless, even your enemies speak your name with respect. Even Nero is afraid of you, Hadria. And not without reason."

She regards me with unveiled surprise. I wonder if I've overstepped, but she simply nods slowly, considering my words.

"You may be right," she finally admits, eyes distant in thought.

I feel a spark of hope that perhaps Hadria will reconsider her relentless drive for power. I understand it—but I fear that bottomless hole of *need* inside her will only destroy her if she lets it.

Wanting to turn our talk to lighter subjects, I say, "You know, I've been thinking about expanding the night garden. There's a section in the west corner that would be perfect for a climbing arch of jasmine or hyacinth."

I describe my plans for the garden, hands sketching shapes

in the air, carried away by my enthusiasm. Hadria listens with a hint of a smile playing about her lips. Though gardening holds little interest for her, she seems content to indulge my passionate monologue about soil pH levels and optimal sunlight gradients.

The night deepens as we talk. Reflecting Hadria's nocturnal schedule, it's nearly 3 a.m. by the time we regretfully roll out of bed. Hadria checks her phone, sighing at the messages waiting for her, all of them silenced and ignored during my time here.

She really has focused solely on me.

If things could be like this all the time, maybe...maybe I *could* find a way to be free here, with her, despite everything.

Suddenly she seems to shift gears, her voice regaining that imperious tone as she announces, "Your mother is coming to visit tomorrow. She'll arrive just after sunset in respect of our customs."

I pause in gathering my clothes together, almost startled. "My mother? I almost forgot! Thank you," I say fervently, throwing my arms around Hadria.

She seems taken aback by the depth of my gratitude over such a simple thing, a faint tinge of color in her pale cheeks when I pull back. For all her power, and for all the times we've made love together, Hadria always seems discomfited by open displays of appreciation, as if unsure how to respond.

She turns away quickly, and I know that the intimacy we shared through these last few hours is over again, over until the next time our desires make us lose control. "You should make sure you get enough rest before she arrives," Hadria says gruffly after a pause. "I know you're not a night owl, not really. Not like me." She sounds almost forlorn...if a crime lord could ever sound forlorn.

I move towards the door. But some reluctant force stays my steps, and I linger a moment longer.

"Thank you," I say simply. "For allowing my mother to visit. It means a great deal to me."

Hadria nods. "I know you've felt isolated here. It seemed prudent to allow some connection to your past life."

There is a clinical distance to her words that rankles slightly.

Hadria is Hades once more.

And I am once again her captive.

How is it that I keep forgetting my place when she reminds me of it so often?

Suddenly exhausted, I make my way out and head back to my own room. The hallways are hushed, only a few house staff moving silently about their tasks. I arrive at my own chambers just as the clock ticks over to 3:19.

I give a hollow laugh when I realize that 3:19 a.m. is actually early for my bedtime now—*very* early. I usually go to bed only when the dawn turns into light. But having spent so much time with Hadria—having spent so much emotional energy—I'm tired.

I'm tired of it all. Tired of the push and pull, the way she runs hot and cold all the time.

So I complete my bedtime rituals with mechanical detachment, brushing out my hair and donning a silk nightdress. And then I lie down and luxuriate for a time in the comfort of the bed, its velvet softness a far cry from the lumpy mattress I had at home. My father always scoffed at spending money on frivolities like furnishings, not when there were debts to be paid and horses to bet on.

Here, I want for nothing material.

But I would still trade all the luxuries in a heartbeat for one day of true freedom, something I've never had.

I turn over and snuggle into the blankets, letting their softness envelop me as completely as Hadria did just a few hours ago. And when I inhale deeply, I catch Hadria's scent still lingering on my skin and in my hair.

I need to stop…doing whatever it is that I'm doing with her. I need to remember that she's the *enemy*.

Tomorrow. My mother will be here tomorrow.

She might be my last chance for freedom.

CHAPTER 27

Aurora

TREPIDATION AND EXCITEMENT war within me as I pace the foyer, awaiting my mother's arrival. My hands smooth over the blush-colored dress I chose with care to make my complexion seem brighter. The rouge I dusted on my cheeks can only do so much to hide the pallor brought on by endless days of night. But I need to appear healthy and thriving. I can't have Mama fussing over me in Hadria's presence.

I need Hadria to remain convinced I'm content to stay here. Hadria, who said she would let me welcome my mother myself, since she had work to finish up.

But I suspect she's probably watching me on one of the many hidden cameras around the house. I know there are a lot of them, because she always seems to know exactly where I am, where I've been. Just one more way to keep me under observation.

On the video monitor by the door, I watch the sleek town car pull up at the gate, sent by Hadria to collect Mama so that my father couldn't sneak in with her this time. A few moments later, gravel crunches beneath tires, and I fling open the front door. The car comes to a stop, and Mama emerges. The sight of her beloved features, so like my own, steals my breath. Laugh lines crease the corners of her eyes and mouth, souvenirs from a happier time before gambling debts and ravenous card sharks consumed our family. Before my father's desperation ensnared me.

I rush down the steps and into her arms, crying out like a child. "Mama!"

She clutches me tightly, only to push me back, holding me at arm's length. Her gaze sweeps over me, and I pray the dress and artful makeup have done their work. But shadows still pool in the hollows of my cheeks, impossible to disguise fully. Something sorrowful flickers in Mama's eyes, but she forces a smile.

"Let me look at you, darling." She brushes back the hair from my forehead, a familiar, comforting gesture. "You look..."

When she trails off, I supply brightly, "Happy? Hadria ensures I want for nothing." Taking her hand, I guide Mama toward the garden. "We have some time before dinner, and Hadria said I could show you my haven here in Elysium."

We descend the manor steps into the night garden's wonderland of exotic blooms. The moon is waning tonight, so the garden isn't at its full beauty, but my mother is still entranced. It's hard not to be. Nodding moonflowers unfurl along the path, luminous petals stretched wide in welcome. I pluck a blossom and tuck it behind her ear, eliciting a smile at last from her worried face.

"Oh, Aurora, this place is magical!" Her voice hitches on the last word. She turns toward me, eyes glinting with unshed tears. "But I can see you're unhappy. I...I'm so sorry."

My smile falters and I press a quick finger to my lips. I guide Mama to a stone bench and as we sit, I clutch her hands, willing my voice to remain steady.

"Please don't cry. I'm safe here." I repeat the well-practiced line loudly enough for anyone listening to hear, ignoring the tightness in my chest. "Hadria treats me well."

"That woman has only locked you away!" Steel edges her words. "No matter how luxurious, this place is still a cage."

I drop my gaze to my hands, twisted in my skirt. "No, Mama, it's not so bad as you imagine. My quarters are lovely, I lack for nothing—"

"Except freedom." My mother tilts my chin up sharply. Her eyes pierce mine, full of fire. "I see the truth, Aurora. You're pale as these moon blossoms. She doesn't let you out during the day, does she? She keeps you in darkness—all the time—" Her voice cracks.

I nod mutely, not trusting my voice, though I wonder how she guessed so easily. But I have to speak. I have to. My only chance is to plan something with Mama, ask her to find a way to raise enough money for a ticket somewhere.

Because I know I can't stay in Chicago when I leave Elysium. Nowhere in the city will be safe. "Mama," I begin, so softly that she has to lean in to hear me, "you need to be careful about what you say. There are always people listening."

Her stern expression crumples and she pulls me fiercely into her arms. "My poor darling, condemned to endless night." Her tears dampen my shoulder. "I should have protected you. Can you forgive me?"

I make soft hushing sounds, stroking her hair. This is really not how I imagined tonight would go. Drawing back, I meet her eyes. "I'm stronger than I realized. Than you and Father ever realized. And Hadria has been kind to me."

Mama recoils, eyes flashing. "*Kind?* She's poisoned your mind, that monstrous devil."

I wince. Monster, devil…I used to think those things myself of Hadria, but now the words seem like a betrayal of my growing connection with her.

Sensing my withdrawal, Mama squeezes my hands, face softening. "Forgive me. This reunion should be a happy one. My little dreamer." She tucks the moonflower behind my ear instead. "You always did believe in making wishes come true. And now, by some miracle, we're together again."

"Yes, I wished with all my heart to see you. And here you are." I take a breath, about to raise the topic I really wanted to talk to her about, but I can't yet find the words. "It's good to see you," I finish awkwardly.

Why can't I do it? Why can't I ask my mother to help me find that freedom she herself said I deserved? If she could get together some money, even over a few years, enough for me to get out of Chicago, then maybe I could do what Hadria did. Disappear and survive on the streets. I can take care of myself now, I know how to fight—

But Mama is glancing around the shadowy garden, and when she looks back to me, I see something terrible in her eyes. "I'm so sorry," she says again.

"It's not your fault."

"Yes it is," she says in the same undertone I used when warning her to watch her words. "Oh, God, yes it is. I'm so sorry, darling, but you being here...it *is* my fault."

I pull back a little. "What do you mean?"

Her eyes dart nervously away from mine, and she unconsciously moves to find a shadow, so that her expression is hidden from me. "The tiara," she half-whispers, half-mouths.

"You gave it up to Hadria long ago, to protect me—" She shushes me, though I spoke softly.

"Yes," she says. "But then..." She sucks in a deep breath. "When your father arranged for you to be married to Nero, I was desperate. I didn't want you to suffer the same life I have suffered. And so I..." She swallows. "I came here to hire the Styx Syndicate. I'm not even sure what I wanted them to do. Kill Nero? Pay off your father's debts? Or...remove him completely..."

My heart is racing. Only a few months ago, my mother so freely admitting to wanting my father dead would have shocked me, despite his cruelty, despite the way I know he treats her.

But now...now I understand.

"What happened?" I ask when she stops.

"I was invited here, to Elysium. I was told I would be granted an audience with Hades. And I was taken into that dark room, the one with the throne, and saw a woman sitting there—the same woman who had come to collect your father's debts all those years ago..." She clenches her jaw. "And she was wearing the tiara, Aurora. She was *wearing* it."

I picture it in my mind. I know how scary Hadria can be, and I can just imagine the cold look on her face when my mother entered the war room.

Mama goes on. "Some wild woman had escorted me in—" Lyssa, that must have been "—and gave me a little shove, told me to—to kneel. So I did. God help me, I did, because I was desperate, and I still didn't understand. I knelt down and Hadria *smiled*, the same horrible smile I remembered from that day she came to threaten your father, and she asked me if I had finally realized who she was. And I did, then. I realized that all those years ago, I'd given up my tiara to Hades herself—and that by contacting her again now, I was only making a deal with the devil. But I *had* to. I couldn't let you go to Nero."

I take her hand, squeeze it. "And I'm *grateful*," I insist. "I'm so grateful—"

But Mama shakes her head insistently. "You still don't understand, Aurora. I bargained with her. Told her she could have you —keep you—as long as you were safe from Nero. And she told me that if she did what I asked, that you could never see the sunlight again, because it would be too dangerous. She told me if I really wanted her to save you, I'd have to agree to your staying with her *forever*. In darkness, forever." She catches her breath. "I didn't understand, Aurora. I thought she meant..."

"Metaphorical darkness," I supply for her.

She nods. "She took off the tiara and gave it to me and told me to think hard about what I was asking. And she said, if I still wanted her help, to put this tiara on you for your wedding day, as a sign. A signal. And I...I did."

I can feel my heart tightening up as I think all this through. "Yes," I say slowly. "You did. But where is it now? Hadria pulled off my veil, along with the tiara—" Inside, I'm wondering if this is my key to freedom. That tiara could certainly cover fake I.D. and a ticket out of the city—or even country.

"After they took you, your father found it with your veil on the ground outside the chapel," she says, voice trembling. "He had to give it to Nero, since..."

"Since I was supposed to cover his debt, and I was gone," I finish. I let go of my mother's hands. "I see."

It's hopeless. I see that now. It was always hopeless to expect someone else to save me—some unseen spirit, or Hadria, or my mother.

If I want my freedom, I can't wait for someone else to grant it to me.

I need to *take* it.

I stand and give a bright smile. "We should go back to the house. I'm sure you're hungry."

But my mother's face darkens as she looks up at me. "You blame me."

"I don't." It's the truth, but Mama doesn't believe me. A strange gentleness comes over me. "Mama, I don't blame you. *You* blame you, and you need to forgive yourself. But I'm not angry with you. Now, please, come back to the house."

But the closer we get to the house, the more upset my mother becomes, until she pulls away from me near the door. "I should go."

"You've barely been here an hour," I say, but I already know she's made up her mind. She stares at me with large, wet eyes, and I take pity on her. "Alright," I say. "Come this way, to the foyer. And I'll ask for the car to come around for you."

I leave her there in the foyer as I head to a side room to contact the garage—here at Elysium, there's a fully-stocked garage housing multiple cars, motorbikes, and even a minivan. But on my way back in from asking for a car to take my mother home, I pause, hearing voices drift in from the foyer—Mama's impassioned tone and Hadria's chill timbre.

On impulse, I quiet my footsteps, slide up against the wall, and listen in.

"...thankful that I allow you to see her at all," Hadria is saying.

"But you can't keep treating her this way! She needs more freedom—she needs *light*." Mama's words are heated, tinged with desperation.

Hadria's cool reply raises the hairs on my arms. "You forget yourself. You gave up any say in her life when you put that tiara on her head."

I creep closer to the door and peek around. Mama has her back to me as she faces off with Hadria. At Hadria's curt reminder, Mama seems to fold in on herself.

"Yes," she says miserably. "Yes...I know. But I didn't know—"

"Yes, you did. You came to a mercenary seeking help. You always knew that help would have conditions. I was perfectly honest with you, Sylvia, and I will keep my promise. Your daughter *will* be safe as long as she remains here at Elysium. As long as she follows my rules and obeys me."

My pulse thuds in my ears, and then I hear the tell-tale crunching gravel as the town car pulls up in front of the house again.

After a fraught beat, Mama says, "Please give Aurora my love and tell her I had to take my leave. If I stay any longer, I'll try to take her with me...and we both know how that would end."

"Oh, yes. We do." A chill goes through me at the unspoken implication. "I'll tell her you love her. Safe travels, Sylvia."

I creep forward, peering around the doorway carefully. Mama moves toward the front door, shoulders slumped. At the threshold she pauses, half-turning. "Please...keep her light from being extinguished by this wicked world you've built."

Hadria says nothing, but I know her well enough by now to understand that the rigid set of her shoulders indicates irritation. And then Mama goes outside without a backward glance.

The great front doors boom shut, echoing with finality.

CHAPTER 28

Hadria

I'M NOT EXACTLY in a hurry to give Aurora her mother's message, to tell her that Sylvia scampered off without bothering to say goodbye, so when I check the cameras to discover Aurora's location, I take my time. And then I walk to Aurora's room much more slowly than I normally would. And when I arrive, I pause for a moment.

This is my house. And Aurora is my captive. But she's more than that now, even I have to admit that. And she deserves at least the impression of privacy.

So I rap my knuckles gently against her door instead of just walking straight in. "Aurora? It's me."

No response.

Alright, I've been as polite as I'm going to be. I turn the handle and step inside. Aurora stands by the shuttered window, her back to me. She doesn't turn, doesn't acknowledge my presence.

She's in a set of fluffy pajamas that are a little too big for her, and for some reason, it makes my heart ache a little to see the way her cuffs pool over her feet, cover her hands, leave only her toes and fingertips on show.

She looks so small. So fragile.

I clear my throat. "I'm sorry, but your mother had to leave. She asked me to tell you she loves you."

Still, Aurora remains frozen in place, staring at the window as though she can somehow see *through* those metal shutters on the outside. An uneasy prickle runs through me at her uncharacteristic detachment.

I take a cautious step forward. "Aurora…did your mother say something to upset you before she left?"

Finally, she turns to me, her gaze guarded. "I just…" Her voice trails off and she looks away, looks at the shuttered window again.

I've never seen her like this—so closed-off, reticent. Aurora has always worn her heart on her sleeve, open and earnest even in her defiance. This…this unsettles me.

I wet my lips. "If your mother—"

"She told me that she was the one who set it up. The kidnapping," she clarifies, finally turning to meet my eyes. Those clear blue eyes of hers are steel now, hard and cold. "She hired you to take me. She thought she was saving me. She doesn't think that anymore, though."

I stand very still. Hearing her speak so plainly of her own kidnapping jars me. Makes it impossible to gloss over the ugly truth with pretty euphemisms.

An unfamiliar heat creeps up the back of my neck. I drop my eyes from hers, fixing them on the cream carpet. "She asked me never to tell—" I stop myself. What difference does it make whether I kept my word to Sylvia Verderosa?

The fact remains that Aurora is here against her will.

I force myself to look at her again. "I'm sorry. Truly. I never meant to…hurt you." The last words come out hoarse. I'm not used to apologizing, and I'm even less accustomed to thinking I might have been wrong about something. "And it wasn't just your mother's request that made me…" Well, that's not any better. I change tack. "I know what my brother is like. And I agreed with your mother—giving you up to him would have been unthinkable."

Aurora presses her lips together and I can see her retreating back into that walled-off space, shutting me out again. She turns away, presenting her shoulder. "She was trying to protect me, I suppose. In her own misguided way. Just like you."

Does she mean *I* am misguided, too?

I yearn to reach for her, to turn her back around and reconnect. But there's an ugly, roiling part of me that wants to remind her she should be *grateful* to me. And I'm not sure which part of me would win out if take her in my arms right now.

"Why don't I have Mrs. Graves bring you something?" I suggest in a strangled voice.

Aurora shakes her head, her dark blond waves swaying with the motion. "No, thank you. I think I'd just like to be alone for a while."

My heart sinks but I nod. "Of course. I'll leave you be." I turn to go when her soft voice stops me.

"Hadria?"

I glance back, hope fluttering in my chest. "Yes?"

She meets my gaze again, some of the hardness gone. "I just wanted to say...thank you. For taking me away from there. From him."

It's exactly what I wanted to hear her say, just a moment ago. But it feels wrong. It feels all wrong, and I don't know why.

She stares down at her hands as she picks at a non-existent loose thread on her pajama pants. "I know I didn't have a choice in coming here. But strange as it sounds, you were the answer to my prayers."

I blink at that, certain I've misheard. "Your...prayers?"

"When my father told me he was marrying me off to Nero Imperioli, I prayed for someone to save me. And you did." The barest ghost of a smile tugs at her rosebud lips. "So thank you."

I stand rooted to the spot, stunned into silence. Since the day I marched into that church and stole her away, Aurora has been my captive. And I have done my level best to remind her of that —to remind her that she will never be free, never leave Elysium.

That she could look upon me as a savior, instead of what I really am...it shakes me to my core. Before I can scrape together any semblance of a response, Aurora runs a hand through her hair. "Anyway, I'm tired. I still can't get used to these topsy-turvy days and nights. So I think I'll just turn in, if that's alright."

She wants me to go. Needs time to process everything. I can give her that, at least.

I move forward and turn down her bedcovers, plumping the pillows the way I've seen Mrs. Graves do for me. She gives me a curious look but doesn't object when I gesture for her to get in. Once she's nestled under the soft covers on her side, I smooth them over her shoulder and pause to dim the bedside lamp.

"Sleep well," I murmur. On impulse, I brush the hair back from her face. Her eyes flutter closed at the contact, and then I bend over and press my lips to her temple. She gives a happy hum.

I have to force myself to withdraw and make my exit.

At the door, I glance back just once. Aurora lies on her side, face peaceful in sleep. Something warm stirs in my chest at the sight. With a soft click, I pull the door closed behind me.

I spend the night with only half a mind on business, earning irritation from Lyssa, who also wants to know why Aurora wasn't at the training session with the other recruits. I make some half-hearted excuse for her that I know will only further convince Lyssa that my getting close to Aurora was a bad idea, but I don't have the energy to argue with my Wolf tonight.

Because yes, maybe it was a bad idea, but I can't change it

now. Don't *want* to change it. Aurora's words play over and over in my mind. She thought of me as her savior. I was the answer to her prayers.

Me. The monster who put her in chains.

And despite all the lies I told myself, I have been cruel to her in her time here. Cruel and—and *mean.* I might not have physically hurt her, but I sure as hell did a number on her psyche.

The hour grows closer toward dawn. Usually I would be thinking about bed around now, with the sun just beginning to turn the sky from black to gray. Instead, I find myself heading to her room again, after sending instructions down to the kitchen.

This time, when I knock gently at her door, she responds with a sleep-husked "Come in."

I enter to find her sitting up in bed, yawning. She looks at the clock and then gives me a quizzical look. "Isn't it late for you to be up?"

I allow myself a small smile. "I hear most people sleep through the night hours, just like you have. I thought it might be fun to see how the other half live. See what the daytime has to offer, since it's so popular." I move to the window and pull the curtains back fully, allowing sunshine to spill across the room. Aurora squints against the unfamiliar brightness, and then gasps.

"The shutters! They're—"

"I had them opened."

"But..." She runs to the window and stares down with hungry eyes at the grounds below.

"Today, you may spend as much time as you like outdoors, in the gardens, in the sunlight."

Aurora's eyes go wide, uncertainty shadowing her face as she turns back to me. In this gentle morning light, I can see how drawn she really looks, and I curse myself for it. "But," she says again, "I thought you didn't want me wandering the grounds during the day. In case someone saw."

"Nero already knows exactly where you are. And if he wants to spy on you to torture himself, well—I'll be happy to provide him the opportunity."

I watch as she slides on a pair of slippers and pulls her robe tight around her. She's too thin, and those clothes are much too big for her, though they'll have to suffice for now. I make a mental note to take her shopping again soon for some pajamas. And perhaps some sundresses. Pretty things to wear while tending the gardens.

"I thought we could have breakfast on the terrace," I say casually, and the way her eyes go wide makes me want to laugh. "If you think you'd like that."

"Yes. Yes, please."

I lead her down through the kitchen and out onto the back terrace. The table is already set for two, with pastries and tea at the ready. I pull out Aurora's chair, earning another curious look. She murmurs her thanks as she takes a seat.

I settle across from her and pour each of us a steaming cup of coffee. God knows I'll need it if I'm to stay up so late past my usual bedtime. Aurora adds a dash of cream and sugar to hers before cradling the cup in her hands. She closes her eyes as she sips, savoring the flavor along with the morning sun on her face. A small hum of satisfaction escapes her.

It's the same noise she makes when I touch my lips to her throat.

She gazes out at the grounds bathed in morning light. "Everything looks so different in the daytime."

"It's a nice change of pace." I sit back, content to watch the interplay of emotions on Aurora's face as she takes in this new view of her surroundings. The way the sunlight brings out the honey tones in her hair, turning her skin golden. She looks so at home here amidst the flowers and fountains.

As if she was always meant to be at Elysium. With me.

But not in the darkness.

Aurora turns her attention back to me and catches me staring. She smiles softly and reaches across the table to lay her hand over mine. "Thank you, Hadria. Truly." Her eyes glisten. "This means…more than you know."

I curl my fingers around hers, giving a gentle squeeze. "You deserve to feel the sunshine on your skin. I'm sorry it's been so long."

We linger like that for a moment, hands entwined, gazing at one another. Aurora breaks the spell first, slipping her hand from mine with a self-conscious tuck of her hair behind her ear.

"Aurora, I—" I stop, unsure how to continue. I want to say so much but the words clog in my throat.

She glances up and gifts me with a tremulous smile. "It's alright. I think I understand what you want to say." She reaches for my hand again, more tentative this time. When I thread my fingers through hers, she exhales softly. "This—being here with you in the morning sun—is enough for now."

Words seem inadequate for the change taking hold between us. As we eat, sharing pastries, savoring the buttery crumbs, I feel a rare sense of peace settle over me.

And before long, the sun climbs higher, chasing away any lingering chill of night. I stifle a yawn behind my hand. "I should probably get some sleep," I say with mild reluctance.

Aurora nods. "Of course. Thank you again for breakfast. And for the gardens. I can't tell you what this all means to me."

I wave off her enthusiasm with feigned nonchalance, secretly pleased. "Yes, well...try not to spend the whole day digging in the dirt, hmm?"

She laughs, and the sound lifts my spirits in a way I can't explain. "No promises," she teases.

I lean back in my seat for a few more moments as I watch Aurora put down her cup of coffee and descend the stone steps, making a beeline for her beloved flower beds. Watching her roam freely across the grounds leaves me feeling both happy and strangely vulnerable. Like I've given up some measure of control.

As if she might just walk out the front gates and never return...

Alone again, I gaze out over the grounds bathed in sunshine. My world seems different in the daytime, changed in some indefinable way. Perhaps it's just that I'm not used to this unusual light as it casts familiar vistas in a new hue.

Or perhaps the change lies within me, wrought by the presence of a radiant young woman who prayed for a monster to save her.

The ruthless Hades, undone by innocence and light. What would my enemies and allies say if they could see the effect Aurora has had on my ice-cold heart? I bark out a short, humorless laugh.

Love is not for people like me. And yet...

The problem, of course, is that this isn't love. Can't be. Not while she is my prisoner.

Not while I'm keeping her here against her will.

CHAPTER 29

Aurora

I'VE NEVER FELT MORE alive at Elysium than I have today.

I spend all day out in the garden, though around an hour after Hadria left me, I ran inside to get a hat and beg some sunglasses from a housemaid. I'm not used to the *light*. My eyes feel weak, my skin burnishing too quickly even in the gentle hours of the morning.

But I have never been so happy in my time here as I was today. Never felt more cherished, more understood, more...

More loved, maybe.

I think everything will be alright. I think, if Hadria can temper that iron will of hers, allow me the things that I need...

I need my freedom. And I still want it.

But Hadria's right. While Nero still seeks me—while he still lives—I can never be free, not really. I can never live without looking over my shoulder. Those silly ideas I had to run away, live on the streets—it would only make it easier for him to snatch me back again.

No. Until Nero is dead and gone, I'm safest here at Elysium, with Hadria.

By the time the sun is lowering again in the sky, I feel like a whole new person. One day in the sun and I feel energized again, my battery refilled. I run up to my bathroom to wash off the dirt and sweat, and while I'm in there, I think of Hadria, as I have been all day—but in a different way now, with the water sliding over me as gently and warmly as her hands—

My heart speeds up as I stroke gently up my thigh, slide my fingers higher...

But why do this myself when I know Hadria can make me feel ten times the amount of pleasure? I can't stop my naughty smirk, and then the follow-up thought: *Why not?*

Why not go to Hadria, wake her with a surprise, just as she did to me this morning?

And so I do. I towel off roughly and don't bother to dress, only pulling on a rose-pink satin robe, and then I run through the concrete hallways of the house—they seem so much brighter now!—to Hadria's room.

I pause at the door, shyness holding me back for a moment as I wonder which Hadria I'll find today. The cold crime boss Hades? Or the woman underneath, the one who actually does have a heart, no matter how much she likes to pretend she doesn't?

Only one way to find out. I knock loudly, and at Hadria's brisk, "Come in," I push open the door.

She's just gotten out of shower, too, judging by her still-damp hair and the fact that she's only in her underwear, a half-tank bra and a pair of Calvin Kleins.

Oh, God. She's so sexy.

"Aurora," she says in surprise. And then she smiles. "I was just thinking about you."

"I was just thinking about you, too," I tell her, and then I run up and throw my arms around her neck before I can chicken out, planting a solid kiss on her mouth. She catches me, makes it feel graceful and sexy instead of awkward and weird, and before I know it, she's pulling open my robe and pressing me back against the wall, mouth on mine in a searing kiss that I feel down to my toes. Hadria's hands are everywhere, firm and knowing, and I moan as her fingers find the wet heat between my legs, rubbing gently.

"I take it you enjoyed your day in the garden," she whispers against my neck, her voice dark and throaty.

"Mmm-hmm," I purr in response, arching into her touch. "I needed it, so much."

"And now, you need—this?"

I can only manage a breathy moan in response as I tangle my fingers in her damp hair. "Y-Yes, Hadria, please."

She smirks, dark and delicious, and then she's on her knees in front of me, placing soft kisses along my inner thighs, teasing me mercilessly before she reaches my center. "You smell so clean and fresh," she says. "I can't wait to get you dirty again." Her tongue flickers out to tease my clit, and I look down to see that wicked glint in her eyes, the one that says she knows exactly what she's doing to me, and it sends a thrill straight through my core.

"Tell me what you want, Sunshine," she demands, her voice like hot honey. "Tell me *exactly* how you want me to make you scream."

"Fuck me with your tongue," I breathe out, looking down at her with lust-hazed eyes. "Take me. *Please.*"

Her tongue laps at my clit again and I throw my head back against the wall, my hips bucking forward. She's *too* good at this, too good at making my knees shake and my clit buzz. She pulls my leg up, throws my thigh over her shoulder, so that I'm spread wide, and then her tongue finds my entrance and slides in, just as I asked.

I whimper with need as she works it in and out of me. It's only been a day since we last did this, so how is it possible I already want it so badly?

"You like that?" she asks with a low chuckle, pulling back to look up at me.

"Yes," I moan. "God yes."

She grins up at me before leaning back in again, pushing deeper this time, her nose rubbing into my clit as she feasts on me. My mouth falls open in a silent 'o', every nerve ending on fire, and then she replaces her tongue with two fingers, setting a quick pace, lapping over my clit rhythmically until I'm seeing stars. The room spins a little bit from the sensations as she crooks the fingers inside me and finds—*oh*—that spot that makes me tingle all over. I can't take much more of this. There's no choice but to come soon.

And then she stops.

"Hadria," I moan out, slapping at the wall, practically climbing her face, trying to wrestle her back into me with my legs. "Hadria, please."

But she just chuckles, kissing along my thighs before standing up slowly, never breaking eye contact with me as she pulls me toward the bed. "You'll get it, I promise. But I want more of you, Sunshine."

She strips off her underwear and then pushes me stomach-down on the bed, spreading my buttcheeks open, and before I can even protest, she's tonguing me *there*, making me squeak and wriggle at the sensation. "Oh, God," I hiss out, as she works her hand underneath me, teasing my clit again. "Hadria!"

That tongue of hers is working into me, and I can't believe how good it feels, how *right* it feels. I want to protest, but it feels *so good* that I just lie there and take it, moaning loud enough that I worry even the soundproofing of the house won't be enough to hide what's happening here in Hadria's bedroom.

"You're so wet," she purrs, her voice practically dripping with need. "I need to taste you again. I want to drown in you." She pulls back, slaps my butt sharply, and says, "Up!"

My groan sounds like a protest, and maybe it is—she's made

me feel so good with what she's been doing, I don't want it to stop.

"Straddling me, Aurora," she commands in a dark, not-to-be-disobeyed voice. "Now. I want you on my face."

I mean...that sounds good, too. So with a whimper, I do as she says. The way she's snapping at me, so autocratic and filthy at the same time, makes me want to do anything, *be* anything she tells me. She lies back on her pillows and pulls me up to sit on her face, grabbing at the monolithic headboard, panting and wriggling. And then she seizes my hips, grinding me hard into her mouth, so that her teeth graze over my clit in a warning, and I stop wiggling around and let her take the lead.

Hadria's tongue slides straight into me and I gasp, feeling it twist and turn, probing and circling, making me feel like I'll combust if she doesn't give me more. "Come on," I pant out, but she just grins against my folds, I can feel it. "Please," I beg, voice breaking slightly. She thrusts her tongue in again, gets a hand around to press against my clit, and my back arches so far I think it might break—

How does she know exactly what I need?

She slaps my ass again until I'm bucking against her mouth, until I can't stop my hips snapping onto her face as she eats me out with a precision that seems almost infernally precise. Her other hand slides between my cheeks to finger me further, tracing the pucker that she was tonguing before, until I'm begging for her to *do it, yes, please*—

The soaking surrounds provide more than enough slick for her to get her fingertip into my ass with ease, right up to the second knuckle, sending out electric waves of pleasure that cascade through my entire body. I've never felt anything like this before, never imagined physical pleasure could be *this* good, that I could feel so full and so...

Complete.

"Come for me, Sunshine," Hadria growls, her lips moving my

clit. "Soak me." Her finger pumps in and out of my ass as her tongue swirls around my clit, sending me over the edge in a blinding orgasm that leaves me trembling and gasping for air. My muscles contract around her invading digit, squeezing hard as I come all over her, crying out as she laps up every drop of me.

At long last, it's too sensitive, too much, and I push away, falling back onto the bed. "Good girl," she murmurs against my skin, pulling me onto her body so we're chest to chest. "Now lie here," she tells me, "just like this so I can ride you until I'm done." She pulls my thigh between her legs and starts thrusting against me, her wet heat coating me. "Oh God, Aurora," she gasps, her hips working frantically. "I spent all night dreaming about doing this to you." She comes fast, with a full-body shudder that leaves her breathless and laughing, and then she hugs me close to her, stroking my hair.

We lie there like that for a while, drowsily kissing and smiling at each other, until Hadria rubs her eyes and says, "What time is it? Staying up to see the sun messed up my internal clock."

I give a huge yawn. "Late. Early. Who knows? But I think I need to sleep."

She lets me lay back against the pillows, propping herself up on her elbows to smile down at me. "I think you do, too." But then something changes in her smile, something that sets off a faint alarm bell in the back of my mind.

"What is it?" I ask, reaching out to take her arm. "Hadria... what is it?"

She swallows. "Aurora," she says softly, and I know whatever she's about to say won't be good news, "I...regret the things I have done to you during your time here." She sees the expression on my face. "Not the sex," she adds quickly. "Well—not the pleasure it's brought you, at least, though really, I shouldn't have..." Her face twists in frustration, and she gets out of the bed, pulling on her robe from where it lay over the back of a chair.

Hadria paces the room, struggling to find the right words as I sit up in bed, dread pooling in my gut. "I've done you a great disservice, Sunshine. I was cruel to bring you here, to keep you prisoner, to keep you in the dark—and most of all, I was cruel to induct you into the Syndicate's business." She turns back to me at last, her eyes full of remorse. "You deserve so much more. A chance at a normal life, away from all this darkness. But I've been dazzled by you, so bright and beautiful. I wanted to possess that light for myself."

"You can have it," I say in a small voice. "You can have it all, Hadria. You can have *me*." You already do, I want to add. But I fear I'll break into a million pieces if I make myself that vulnerable.

She gives a pained sigh. "Sunshine, don't you see? I can't keep you here. As much as it pains me...I *need* to set you free." She comes and sits on the edge of the bed, taking my hands in hers. "I want you to have that freedom you crave."

"But I—I don't—"

"Aurora," she says, not sharply, but desperately, as though this conversation is costing her everything. "Don't you see? While I keep you here against your will, I can never really be certain if...if this thing between us..." She trails off.

"It's real," I assure her after a moment. "Believe me, Hadria. It's real."

Her smile is twisted. "But you can't know that, Sunshine. Not until you've had the opportunity to experience something different. Your whole life, you haven't had a choice. And I want to be the one to give you that. To give you the choice to stay...or leave." She holds up a hand as I open my mouth to tell her that I choose to stay. "But you need time to yourself, to think it through. You owe yourself that. So please...listen to my proposal."

CHAPTER 30

Aurora

AS HADRIA LAYS out her idea, I begin to understand: my prayers have been answered again.

My wishes have been granted.

And at first I would give anything to take back those prayers and those wishes.

I'll be given the choice of freedom, true freedom, with all the money I could ever need, and a fake passport and a blank plane ticket to anywhere in the whole world. "You'll stay in my safe house downtown," Hadria says, "for one week. I'd make it longer, Sunshine, but I...I don't think I can cope with more than a week of uncertainty. Because I have to *know*. I have to know that, between me and everything else this whole world has to offer, you would really and truly choose me."

"But Nero—"

"Doesn't know where this place is. And no one will know you are there; it's my personal fortress. You will have everything that you need there. There's a gym and a pool, a sauna, a spa...it won't be true freedom while you're there, I grant you. You'll need to stay in the apartment, never go out to the streets, because it would be too dangerous without eyes on you."

"You won't...have people following me?" I ask slowly.

She shakes her head.

Now that *is* tempting. In my time here at Elysium, I've become used to being under observation at all times. I barely even bother to pick out the spies trailing at my heels these days, or play spot-the-camera in the house.

"It would be a risk," Hadria goes on. "You need to understand that. Here at Elysium, there's no way Nero could touch you. Out there—even in the safe house—I can't guarantee your safety."

I can see how much it's costing her to offer this. She can barely force the words out, barely admit that she is willing to let go of control enough to put me into some small risk.

And my first reaction, to my own irritation, is fear. Fear that Nero will find me, that I'm being cast out of the nest with no safety net. For a second, I'm once again that naive little fool who just accepted everything happening to her without the slightest resistance, who never stood up for herself, who never *fought* for herself.

But I know how to fight these days. And I can't stay bundled up in bubble wrap for the rest of my life.

Or rather...I don't want to.

So I nod, since Hadria seems to expect a response. "It would be a risk. I understand."

"You can spend the week alone, truly alone," she goes on, "and think through everything that has happened to you here. Think about whether..." She swallows. "Whether you might ever be able to forgive me for the things I've done to you."

It's on the tip of my tongue to reassure her at once, to say at once, *of course I can forgive you*, but I bite the words back.

What Hadria is proposing, even though I initially hated the idea, actually makes sense.

"And at the end of that week, if you find that you do want to return to me...then there's a café downstairs in the building opposite. Meet me there at 9 a.m. sharp if you want to return to

Elysium. I'll wait there for an hour. If you don't show, then..."
She gives a shrug. "Then I'll know you've chosen a different fate.
I've already set up a bank account for you." She actually turns
and rummages in her nightstand, then hands me ten brand new
passports, and a card folded up in a piece of paper with typed
instructions. "Your new passports," she says. "Use whichever one
you like and then burn it when you get wherever you want to
go. And that card will give you access to your account. I put a
billion in there for you; I think that should cover it."

I drop the passports I've been flicking through curiously—all
different nationalities: American, Canadian, British, Australian
—to stare at Hadria in shock. "You put *a billion dollars* in an
account for me?" I choke out, picking up the card to look at it,
holding it gingerly by the corners as though it might spontaneously combust.

Hadria gives a nod. "I said I wanted to give you true freedom. I meant it. You can start a brand new life. Be a brand new
person. Hire protection if you ever feel you need it—but I will
put out the story here in Chicago that you have died, so no one
should come looking for you. And of course, I intend to kill
Nero in the next few weeks. So once that happens..." She
shrugs, then gives me a quick glance. "If you wanted to take
your mother with you, I could arrange passports for her, too. Or
I can inform her, privately, that you are alive and thriving else-
where. I believe she'd take that secret to the grave."

"Yes," I say quietly. "Yes, I believe she would." My mother
certainly knows how to keep a secret. "And I think—if I *was* to
start a new life—I think I would go alone."

Mama. I would miss her, certainly. But freedom always has a
cost.

In this case, a billion dollars and a mother, apparently.

"So you'll do it?" Hadria asks softly. "You'll go to the safe
house and...consider?"

I look up at her, feeling my heart crack a little at the thought of leaving her. But I owe it to her, and to myself most of all, to make sure that I'm making the choices I truly want to make.

Without duress.

"Yes," I tell her. "I'll go."

And I do.

I go a few days later, trying not to cry as Hadria drives me herself to the safe house, the same apartment where she took me that first day, where we stopped for only moments.

She takes me up there, shows me around. It's as well-appointed as she promised, though a little...sterile. The books are mostly coffee table books, the kind used for display. But there's a giant TV—several, actually—and she even gives me a phone, telling me I can use the internet as much as I like.

I've never told her this, but I've never owned a phone before. My father wouldn't allow it, and it didn't seem necessary to me, anyway. I had no friends. No one to gossip with over text messages or to envy their amazingly curated lives on social media.

Hadria probably knows it, though, based on the way she walks me through opening the phone, putting in a password, connecting to the Wi-Fi. She acts like this is normal, but I know it's not.

I've never been normal.

That's what I'm coming around to seeing, finally.

"I'll leave you now," she says at last, and I let the tears drip down my face as I hug her goodbye. "Please make the right choice for *you*," she whispers to me. "I want you to be happy. Happy and free, no matter what."

"Please be careful," I beg her. "Please, please be careful."

She hugs me tight for a moment more, then turns and heads

for the door, calling over her shoulder, "I'll be there next Friday morning, Sunshine, at that café across the street. I'll see you then...or I'll remember you always."

She's gone before I can break down and really sob.

———

I spend the week thinking, just like Hadria wanted me to. I spend it thinking of every bad thing at Elysium, from the eternal darkness of the place, to the not-so-nice people there sometimes, to the fact that Hadria is a killer, a criminal, remorseless and ruthless and unlikely to change.

But all of those things fade into the background when I think about how Hadria makes me feel. About the changes that Elysium has wrought in me, about Lyssa's tutelage, about the friends I've made there—because I do consider that group of trainees my friends, now.

I've never had friends before. I've never been able to stand up for myself before Lyssa's lessons.

And I've never felt about someone the way I feel about Hadria.

She really did give me a billion dollars. *A billion dollars.* I checked the account. And I think about all the places I could go with money like that, and all the good I could do in the world, too.

I think hard, all week.

But I already knew my decision even before I arrived here at the safe house, and by the time Friday morning rolls around, it hasn't changed.

I will be returning to Elysium. Returning to Hadria. And...I plan to tell her how I feel about her. Because if there's one thing this week has given me, it's perspective. And I know for sure, now, what it is I feel.

I love her.

I love Hadria Imperioli, with all her faults and flaws, despite all the terrible things she's done in her life, despite what she did to *me*.

I love her. And I want to find a way to forgive her, to erase the bad beginning that we had. I want to find a way to be with her, to shape a life together.

I know it's the right decision because of how calm I feel once I've made it. But as the hour comes closer, the clock ticking over maddeningly slowly, I feel a bubbling joy inside as well. I can't wait to see her. Oh, God, I can't wait.

I run out to the terrace, the huge terrace with a pool that I've spent hours floating in this week, looking up at the blue sky, soaking in the sun, and I look down to the café on the street in the building opposite. I must have had some sixth sense, because I see her, right away—walking down the sidewalk, that catwalk stride she has, stomping her feet and swinging her hips, her fists shoved deep in her leather jacket's pockets. Even from this bird's eye view, she's unmistakable.

And she's *early*. I don't have to wait a single second longer.

I grab my phone—over the last week, it's somehow become indispensable—and I bolt for the door, stabbing impatiently at the elevator button on the landing outside the apartment. I'm on the top floor, and the elevator is a private one, leading down to the lobby.

It's the longest elevator ride of my life. And when I get down there, I'm shoving through the elevator doors before they're fully open, heading for the door to the street—

But there's a man coming in at the same time, a man with the most enormous bouquet of flowers I've ever seen in my whole life. It takes up half his body, so that I can only see his feet and legs, and his hands around the large box from which the flowers are pouring out.

All my favorites. All the flowers from the night garden. Snowdrops and white roses and calla lilies and and baby's breath—

"Ms. Verderosa?" says the man from behind the flowers.

"Yes?" I say.

"These are for you. Lucky I ran into you, these things are an armful! A gift from someone calling herself...Hadria? Is that right? Well anyway, I just need you to sign for them, if you could —" He staggers over to the reception desk. It's never staffed; Hadria told me when she took me here that she chose this place on purpose, since she didn't need someone watching her coming and going.

The delivery man deposits the huge bouquet on the desk and turns to me with an electronic tablet and an expectant look.

"Oh, but I—" I begin, casting a longing look across the road. This was a lovely gesture from Hadria, but she's *right there* in person across the road.

The man's face drops. "Please, ma'am, just a quick signature here—I'm running late this morning already, and it'd really help me out if you could just—"

"Of course," I say quickly. I approach him, looking at the tablet. "I sign on this?"

"That's right. Just use your finger."

I reach out to sign, and as I do, his other hand comes up, and I feel a sharp sting in my arm. "What are you—" I begin, and take a step back, my instincts finally kicking in as I see him throw aside a hypodermic syringe.

The hypodermic syringe he just used to inject me.

No one knew I was here.

And Hadria would *never* be so foolish as to send me flowers here.

I raise up my hands, ready to put my training into action, but my fingers won't seem to close, won't turn into the fists I need...

My head is swimming. No...the whole room is swimming, and I'm going under...

"Nothing personal, you understand," the man says with a cheery smile. "Just business, ma'am. Give it another second and it'll all be ov—"

CHAPTER 31

Hadria

I WAIT a long time at the café.

I told Aurora I would wait only an hour, but I wait much longer than that, buying coffee after coffee that I don't drink, and leave to one side to get cold, get removed, get replaced by a hot coffee that inevitably turns cold.

At one point, the owner comes out to ask me if I ever plan to move along. With a hard stare, I slide three thousand dollars cash across the table to him. "I'll leave when I'm ready," I tell him.

"Yes, indeed, ma'am," he says, his eyes lighting up as he palms the bills. "You stay as long as you like."

But when the late afternoon sun is beginning to die, and the waitstaff have been sent home, and the owner himself is turning away other patrons at the door, telling them that he's shut for the day, I finally have to admit it to myself.

Aurora has made her choice.

She's not coming.

The Underworld Duet concludes in
Consort of the Crime Queen

About the Author

Persephone Black likes Ice Queens who melt behind closed doors, Underworld Empresses who protect what's theirs, and Bad Girls who stay bad to the end...but win the love of a good woman.

Also by Persephone Black

BIANCHI FAMILY DUET

When the reckless street-racing daughter of an Irish Mob Boss is forced to marry the billionaire Ice Queen heiress to a rival Italian Family, forbidden passion ignites between the two women as threats from their dangerous worlds try to tear them apart.

RUBY REALM DUET

When an undercover FBI agent falls for the charismatic Mafia princess she's investigating, she must choose between love and the law. But danger is closing in on both of them…

Printed in Great Britain
by Amazon

39364207R00130